Silent Journey

A Novel by Carl Watson

with illustrations by Andrew Bosley

ONE ELM
BOOKS

Egremont, Massachusetts

One Elm Books is an imprint of Red Chair Press LLC
www.redchairpress.com
www.oneelmpress.com
Free Discussion Guide available online

Publisher's Cataloging-In-Publication Data
Names: Watson, Carl, 1933- author. | Bosley, Andrew, illustrator.
Title: Silent journey : a novel / by Carl Watson ; with illustrations by
Andrew Bosley.

Description: [Egremont, Massachusetts] : One Elm Books, an imprint of Red
Chair Press LLC, [2020] | Interest age level: 009-014. | Summary:
"Following an accident that took his mother's life eight years before,
doctors discovered Scott Schroeder was suddenly deaf. Picking up on
conversations he observes, Scott figures out a big family secret
concerning his father and uncle and makes his mind up to play a part in
their reconciliation"--Provided by publisher.

Identifiers: ISBN 9781947159303 (hardcover) | ISBN 9781947159310
(paperback) | ISBN 9781947159327 (ebook)

Subjects: LCSH: Deaf children--Juvenile fiction. | Family secrets--
Juvenile fiction. | Lipreading--Juvenile fiction. | Gymnasts--Juvenile
fiction. | CYAC: Deaf children--Fiction. | Family secrets--Fiction. |
Lipreading--Fiction. | Gymnasts--Fiction.

Classification: LCC PZ7.1.W4152 Si 2020 (print) | LCC PZ7.1.W4152 (ebook)
| DDC [Fic]--dc23

LC record available at: https://lccn.loc.gov/2019946960

Main body text set in 13/18.5 Bembo

Printed and bound in the United States of America.
0420 1P F20CG

Table of Contents

In memory of Mike, our fun-loving,
but protective German shepherd.

Kansas

Scott Schroeder yanked a can out of the drink machine in front of the gas station. As he fumbled with his change from the slot, a coin fell out of his hand and rolled out into the drive. He stepped to it and bent over to pick it up. A sudden bump from behind sent him sprawling.

Startled but unhurt, he sat up as a large man jumped out of the cab of his truck and trudged toward him.

"You all right?" asked the man, puffing from the exertion.

Scott chastised himself as he thought about his carelessness. *Of all the stupid things to do, this was one of the worst.*

Seeing the kid was fine, the concern on the man's face morphed into anger. "You idiot! You stepped out right in front of my truck!"

Scott's dad ran over from the gas pump where he had been

fueling their car, crouched next to Scott, grabbed him by the shoulders, and stared into his face. "You okay?"

As Scott signed 'OK,' he felt his face turning red. He wished he was an ant and could disappear down a crack in the pavement; that this whole scene had never happened.

Glancing back, his dad gave the driver a furious once-over, shouting, "He's deaf, man! He couldn't hear you!"

The driver's mouth dropped open. "How would I know that?" he yelled. "That boy's gotta watch what he's doing." Pivoting on his heel, the man pounded the pavement, all the way to his truck.

Incensed, Charles Schroeder stood up as if he intended to lunge after him.

Scott had understood the exchange by reading their lips. Pushing himself up, he grabbed his dad's arm, then touching the tips of his hands to his own shoulders, whispered, "My fault."

His dad exhaled as he peered into Scott's eyes. "He *is* right, you know. You have to be more careful."

Scott signed an 'S' for yes without looking up. He usually *was* careful, knowing he had to use his eyes to compensate for his deafness, but he had messed up. Silently, he vowed it would never happen again. He scooped the scattered coins and slid them in his pocket, picked up his drink, and followed his dad into the gas station to buy a couple of snacks.

As the attendant greeted them, Scott acknowledged him

by lifting his hand in a slight wave. The office smelled greasy and the employee looked like he had been spending the morning under the hood of a car.

Beyond the windows, the highway seemed to go on forever. Not wanting to meet the attendant's stare, he thought about the accident that had caused his deafness. He didn't remember much, just flames, heat, shadows, and loneliness. But that was seven years ago when he was six.

Since then, Scott had endured a world of silence. The doctors told him there was nothing physically wrong with him, other than a few cuts and bruises. They had decided that the trauma he had experienced caused his deafness and that time would cure it. Yet, here it was, seven years later, and he still couldn't hear. Maybe the reason he and his dad moved so often was because of his handicap.

Communication was a challenge and his dad had to be gone a lot, but he was very good at lip reading and getting better at it all the time.

Leaving the station, Scott and his dad got back in the car and pulled out onto the highway. The traffic was light; being a Sunday afternoon in early June. Scott fastened his seat belt and dug out a magazine to read about some of his favorite gymnastics heroes.

Right then, his dad hit the brakes as another car cut in front of them. Scott caught a few profane words escaping from his dad's lips.

Smirking, he thought about how his skill at lip reading might be an embarrassment if folks realized he didn't need to hear to understand what they said. As other vehicles passed on the highway, he wondered how loud their sounds might be. His friends on the gymnastics team often grumbled about distracting noises during competitions. Not him.

He opened his magazine and examined the photos of his favorite champions. The pictures showed them proving to the world they could do things others only dreamed about. Several had overcome physical pain and injury. Some were small and strong like him. None were deaf.

Maybe that was an advantage. At home, one of his teammates slipped on the rings during competition when startled by a sudden cheer from the audience. That would never happen to him, but there were times he didn't know an audience was applauding until someone poked him and pointed.

A tap on his shoulder broke into his thoughts. His dad carefully mouthed his words. "You can tell we're in Kansas."

Scott took in the countryside flying by his window. Tall, yellow sunflowers, almost the color of his hair, lined the highway. Beyond the barbed wire fences lay flat fields of ripening grain, dotted with an occasional farmstead. Soon, the combines would roll through the fields and leave behind miles of stubble. He had never seen harvesting take place, but it had been described to him.

Was this to be their new home; a place where he would have to make new friends all over again? He closed his magazine with a sigh, pulled out his pocketknife, and picked up a small block of wood from the floorboard. He thought about asking when the combines would start but decided it would be unwise to distract his dad with hand movements, and he didn't want to 'say' anything. His voice was changing, and the expression on other people's faces let him know when it sounded weird.

His teammates had learned some signing; actually finding it humorous to intimidate their competitors by using his hand gestures to communicate with each other. *Well, why not?* Scott reasoned. *The other teams used their voices so I couldn't understand them unless they were facing me, and then not talking too fast.*

Will I ever be on a team again? He had been told there were no gymnastics teams in Chelsey.

Scott was so deep in his thoughts and memories that a touch from his dad made him jump.

"Not in the car," he said, pointing at the knife.

Scott put the wood back down and returned the knife to his pocket, then watched his dad's face, deciphering as he spoke.

"You'll like it at your grandmother's. But you must understand, she's different from your Aunt Sally. You got along well with your aunt and you can get along with her as well. You just have to remember, she's the matriarch of the family and what she says, goes."

Scott thought about what he had said.

"Son, Chelsey is different from Fort Worth," continued his dad. "It's smaller and there's a stream for fishing that runs right through the middle of town."

Scott signed that he understood, and then looked away, remembering his last home. Why did his aunt have to get married and move all the way to Alaska? They had been staying with her in Texas. Before that, they had lived with his mother's parents, and before that, a cousin. What other few relatives he knew were busy with their own lives. That left no one to pay attention to him.

Well, that was all right. He didn't need a babysitter. His dad said that someday they would have their own home, and he wouldn't have to travel anymore. But that "someday" seemed mighty far off.

His dad just said that Grandmother was a "May-tree-ark." Noah had to use strong, tough wood to build an ark for all the animals. Maybe that meant that a May tree was tough and sturdy. Grandmother, like a May tree, must be the same way.

Receiving a gentle nudge, he glanced up.

"I know it's only June, but the company will let me take a sort of working vacation for a couple of days. We might even be able to do some fishing, but I'll have to check with the office in Wichita on Monday."

He motioned at a city limit sign next to the freeway.

"We're here!"

After several turns, his dad pulled in front of a large two-story house with a covered porch that extended across the front. It had a fresh coat of white paint and the curtains in each window were pulled back exactly the same. The hedges were trimmed in a perfect straight line, and there wasn't a single leaf or twig to mar a well-manicured lawn. And, on top of all that, a colorful bed of petunias waved in the breeze bordering the house.

Scott wasn't impressed. The house was perfect, too perfect. Yet, no high bar existed for him to climb on, not even a swing. Even the branches of the trees were trimmed so high that they would be difficult to climb. His dad said there was less crime in a small town. What he hadn't said was there also might be less to do.

Scott opened the car door and cautiously stepped out. The smell of wildflowers and the warm earth was overwhelming. Across the street, marigolds sprouted in the yard of a house where the paint was peeling on weathered windowsills. The place appeared deserted except for a German shepherd lying on the front landing.

The dog was brown, black, and small for its breed. It looked hungry and lonely, like it had been abandoned.

Scott tugged his dad's coat sleeve and pointed.

"What do you see?"

"A dog," replied Scott, snapping his fingers and softly

using his voice at the same time.

"Now, Scott, I know you like animals, but leave that one alone; at least until you get acquainted with its owners."

Scott shook his head, signing "no" and "one" as he whispered, "No one is there."

His dad noticed the scattered, rolled-up newspapers. "Hmm, you might be right. We'll ask your grandmother." He grabbed his suitcase from the trunk of the car and started toward the house, then turned and waited.

Scott snatched a couple of bags from the back seat, heaved a sigh, and followed him up the sidewalk.

Mrs. Schroeder's housekeeper, Ralston, met them at the door. Tall, thin, and elderly, the corners of the man's mouth turned down in a scowl.

"Hello, Ralston." Mr. Schroeder greeted him with a handshake.

"It is good to see you, sir." Ralston's expression never changed.

Scott studied Ralston's stone-faced appearance. The housekeeper's eyes displayed a faint look of friendship or amusement, he couldn't tell which.

Ralston took their bags to the center of the foyer, set them down, and ushered them into the living room. He left to take their bags upstairs to assigned rooms as Grandmother Schroeder made her stately entrance.

Dressed in a long, black dress and leaning on a cane, she

gave them both a non-committal stare.

"Hello, Mother," his dad said in greeting, then kissed her lightly on the cheek.

"Welcome home, Charles," she replied; her eyes drifting to Scott.

Scott, not knowing what to do or say, remembered watching a science-fiction movie where a scientist studied a new species under a microscope. *Am I being observed in the same way?*

"I see you brought him," she said, never taking her eyes off her grandson. "He has certainly grown since the last time you were here. It's been quite a while. Just how handicapped is he?"

After his dad replied something—he was clueless what, since he had his back to him—she looked at Scott even more intensely and appeared to shout as if she were trying to communicate with an alien. "Hel-lo, Scott!"

Scott bowed slightly in response. All he could think was how much she smelled like a bar of soap and could only imagine what brand it was.

"The resemblance is uncanny," she muttered and intensified her scrutiny.

Scott raised his eyebrows. *I look like Dad, except for the color of my hair. What's so unusual about that?*

"Perhaps the sins of the father are forgiven as visualized in the son," she added, glancing at Scott's dad.

Scott thought he understood her words and scratched his head at the strange comment. *What sins? What does she mean? It makes no sense.*

His dad's countenance saddened as he replied something and turned away. Looking back at his grandmother, Scott decided right then that a May tree must have thorns on it. With that, his attention flew out the window and over to the house across the street.

The dog still lay alone at the front door. As Scott watched, he got slowly to his feet and nuzzled at the empty pan nearby. He circled about a couple of times and lay back down, opening and closing his eyes as if blinking back tears.

The dog had been abandoned. Scott knew all about that. He'd been left to live with one relative after another so often that he had accepted it as a part of his life. Still, his dad couldn't help it if he had to travel. It was his job.

Scott felt a hand on his shoulder. Facing his dad, he snapped his fingers twice to ask if his grandmother knew about the dog.

"My God! Is he both deaf and dumb!?" exclaimed his grandmother.

Scott saw what she said and shouted, "No! Not dumb!"

The shocked look on her face showed Scott that his voice had sounded weird again. His teammates never called him dumb; neither did the kids at school.

His eyes filled with tears as he moved closer to the

window. That dog lying on the landing across the street wouldn't think him dumb just because he used sign language and couldn't hear. He rubbed his arm across his eyes.

A touch on his arm got his attention. With concern clouding his dad's face, he said "Your grandmother apologizes. She didn't mean it the way it came out."

Scott did not want him to see the tears in his eyes, but the pressure of a hand on his shoulder told him there was more, and he had to look back at his dad's face.

"She was really asking if you could talk since she hadn't heard you speak. I explained you felt more comfortable using sign language." Charles took a deep breath and let it out slowly, considering how to put it. "Your grandmother isn't always easy to understand; that is, to know why she says or does some things.

"I asked about the dog. The owner moved away a few days ago and left him. Your grandmother called Animal Control, but they couldn't catch him."

This was upsetting to Scott since he could so relate.

"Scott, he's a stray. She had to call them. And even if you did make friends with him, you can't bring him here." His dad crouched down next to him, holding both of his hands. "Your grandmother is allergic to dogs. She'd never allow one in the house. It might be best to just leave him alone."

Scott scanned the room for his grandmother.

The Ark had left.

A New Friend

That evening, as the sun touched the horizon, Scott slipped into the kitchen. After filling a pan with leftovers from the refrigerator, he stepped out on the front porch and fixed his eyes on the house across the street. The German shepherd rested on the landing at the top of the steps, head between his paws.

Slowly, Scott inched in his direction. The time had come to get acquainted.

The dog glanced up. With suspicion in his eyes, he pointed his ears and stared. When Scott moved to the first step, the dog leaped off the landing and trotted to the corner of the house.

Scott moaned. He knew that gaining his trust wouldn't be easy. After all, he had been abandoned, chased by dog catchers, and starved.

After setting the pan on the landing, Scott retreated to the other side of the street. He sat quietly on the curb, his mind wandering back to the previous morning's mishap at the service station; an experience he intended to erase from his memory.

A movement across the road caught his attention.

The dog had returned to the steps, climbed them cautiously, sniffed at the pan, and hungrily gulped its contents. Satisfied, he turned around three times and lay next to it.

Scott dug into a paper sack and once more advanced, holding a bone in front of him.

A pair of large, dark eyes traced his every move, widening with distrust. Again, the dog hopped off the landing and trotted to the corner of the building.

Scott laid the bone on the bottom step, walked back across the street, and again sat on the curb.

Cautiously, never taking his eyes off Scott, the dog returned to the steps and sniffed around the bone.

His grandmother's porch light came on as his dad opened the door. Scott hopped to his feet, sprinted a few feet, then performed a pair of handsprings and an aerial en route.

"Time to come in," said his dad, signing 'come' with a single quick downward movement of his index fingers.

Scott held up one finger, indicating he would come in a

moment. He wanted to be sure the dog would quiet down for the night.

Charles observed them both, knowing it was hopeless; that Scott loved animals and could not stand to see them suffer. "Okay, but latch the door before you go to bed." He pointed at the door and demonstrated how to secure it.

After his dad stepped back inside, the dog climbed back to the landing above the steps with the bone in his mouth. As before, he turned around three times, then flopped down on the stoop. With the prize between his paws, he shut his eyes as if perfectly content.

Scott sat and studied him a moment; thought about approaching him again but didn't. Perhaps it would be best to wait.

Standing up with a stretch and a yawn, Scott climbed the front steps. Even though he had not yet petted him, he felt certain that the groundwork for a new friendship had begun. After one final glance to assure that his new pal had settled for the night, he went inside, latching the door behind him.

Scott joined his dad in the family room and sat down to watch TV, but without captions, he couldn't understand a lot of it. Instead, he picked out a book that identified various kinds of dogs from a shelf and shook his dad's arm. With a gesture, he placed his hand to his mouth to sign a good night.

"Tired of TV, eh?" he asked, pointing at the book.

Scott nodded.

"I understand. Sleep well."

Scott slid a 'Y' hand shape back and forth in front of him, "You, too." He took the steps two at a time to his bedroom, put on his pajamas, and fell asleep reading about German shepherds.

★ ★ ★

The smell of bacon and freshly brewed coffee filled the air, springing Scott's eyes open the next morning. He sat up and focused on the window, rubbing his eyes.

Anemic shafts of light had begun to sift through an old cottonwood tree that towered above the house. Bewildered for a moment, he then remembered the events of the past evening.

Bolting out of bed, he got dressed and raced down the stairs, cautiously opening the front door and peering across the street.

There he was, right where he last saw him, still lying on the landing. The dog opened his eyes, eyebrows scrunched, and looked directly at him, then struggled to his feet and stretched. Like a majestic lion rising to inspect his kingdom at the dawn of a new day, he scanned the neighborhood. Then, with a defiant flip of the tail, off the steps he jumped, strutting up the street.

At the breakfast table, Scott signed 'good morning' to his

dad and struggled to speak the words to his grandmother. The skin around his dad's eyes crinkled happily as he signed a response. The Ark remained stoically hidden behind a newspaper. Scott didn't know if she had spoken a reply without remembering that he needed to see her lips.

Scott rushed through the meal and tapped on the table to get his dad's attention. He signed 'go' with his hands and pointed outside.

"I'm not so sure about that."

"Please!" Scott begged, making a circular motion on his chest and speaking at the same time. It was a beautiful day, too pretty to be cooped up inside. He begged his dad with his eyes.

"What does he want?" asked his grandmother, laying down the newspaper.

"To roam around the neighborhood, but he doesn't know anyone."

"Let him go. This isn't the city. You're being overprotective. He's thirteen years old and certainly can't be under foot all day like an invalid."

Scott's mouth dropped open. The Ark actually appeared to be on his side. Then it occurred to him that she might only be anxious to get him out of her sight. Because of his deafness, some people seemed uncomfortable around him. He raised an eyebrow to his dad and gave him a special pleading look that nearly always worked.

Charles Schroeder studied him a moment. Finally, he breathed a sigh of resignation. "Scott, there's a park across the way and the city library is a couple of blocks up the street." His dad spoke distinctly, carefully forming the words with his mouth.

Scott understood. He would find them.

"Check out the park. I think it has a pair of monkey bars in it. Whatever you do, don't get near the freeway, and remember to look before you cross the streets, okay?"

"You talk like I am baby!" said Scott, angrily signing 'talk' and cradling his arm like he was holding a baby.

"Sorry," replied his dad, sincerely. "I didn't mean it like that. Just remember, you're all I have."

The anger faded from Scott's face. After all, the reverse was just as true. His dad was all *he* had.

"I have to go into Wichita this morning, but Ralston will be here and so will your grandmother."

Scott made a wheel driving motion followed by a double 'K' sign. "Drive carefully. Remember, you're all *I* have."

"Ha! Touché! Guess I deserved that."

Scott shook his head with the sign for worry. He whispered, "Don't worry. I'll be fine." Racing through the front door, he slammed it shut behind him, and shot down the steps.

How could anyone not *be happy on a day like this?* It was June, the air smelled fresh and clean, the sun shone, and *no* school. He felt like whistling, so he puckered up and blew, then laughed at himself, not knowing what kind of sound, if any, that he made. Running across the front lawn, he did a quick series of cartwheels and ended with a round-off back handspring. *Too bad there's no gym around.* He stuck both hands deep into his pockets and ambled up the sidewalk.

At the park, he headed for a pair of monkey bars next to the swings. One bar was about six feet high; the other appeared to be a couple of feet lower. He shinnied up to the higher one and pulled himself on top of it. The bar was rough and rusty. It was so gross that even a pair of handgrips wouldn't have been of much help.

Dropping to the ground, he made his way to a sycamore, and climbed to one of its upper branches. He looked south across the freeway where hundreds of acres were planted with wheat. Near the horizon, a breeze moved across heads of grain. Like ocean waves, they rippled down the field until they vanished against a hedgerow near the highway.

To the east, the morning sun reflected from a swimming pool where groups of young folks gathered, laughing and splashing about in the water. He wanted to join them but couldn't. Being unsure of the sound of his voice, he dreaded meeting strangers, even with a friend; doing it alone was almost impossible.

Scoping out the area, he saw a familiar shadow. Partly hidden behind an oak tree, his new friend from the night before lay near the edge of a baseball field, watching the freeway. Occasionally, he would rest his head on his paws and blink his large, brown eyes.

There's one who could stand some company. He jumped from the tree and approached the German shepherd slowly with outstretched hand.

At first, the dog looked like he might run again. Scott wished he had some food to offer. Eventually, patience won out, and he allowed Scott to crouch beside him.

"Hi, I'm Scott. Wish you could tell me your name," he whispered, patting his head.

Watching his every move, the dog seemed to decide there was no danger, moved his tail a couple of times, and licked Scott's hand.

Scott had an idea. "Come. I'll find you something to eat." He started walking backwards, slapping a hand on his thigh as an invitation.

The dog's tail whacked the ground, but he didn't seem inclined to move. Instead, he rose into a crouch position and lowered his ears.

Puzzled, Scott continued to step backwards onto a baseball diamond, trying his best to get the dog to follow.

Suddenly, someone grabbed him by the shoulders and shoved. He swung about in alarm to see a tall, lanky boy in a baseball cap, yelling, "You deaf or something? Get out of the way, or we'll give you a little help!"

Frightened, Scott pointed at one of his ears and started to explain when something brushed against his leg. His new friend stood in front of him, facing the boy with his lips pulled back in a snarl, looking as vicious as an enraged wolverine.

The kid got the message and backed off as Scott's mouth dropped open. The dog took a stance in front of him. The other ballplayers on the field apparently noticed the excitement and moved toward them.

The dog, uncomfortable with all the commotion, scoped out the nearest path of escape. Unexpectedly, he bolted, disappearing like a ghost into the shadows of the park.

Scott shifted from one foot to the other. Then, without comment, he took off running in the same direction. He looked everywhere but didn't see the dog anymore that day.

A New Home

The next morning after breakfast, Scott sat on the front porch steps, whittling on a small piece of wood. He had not seen the dog since the incident in the park and wondered where his new friend had spent the night. Regardless, the food had disappeared, so he was probably in the area.

A moving van backed into the yard across the street. Three men got out and started moving furniture and boxes from the back of it into the house.

What in the world is he thinking about all those people invading his home? Suddenly, he saw him. The German shepherd darted across the road and leaped into the cab of the van through a door that had been left ajar.

Closing his knife, Scott slipped it back into his pocket. *What strange behavior!* A large, husky worker appeared in the doorway of the house and shouted something but was too far away for Scott to see what he said.

The man headed back to the van. Almost there, he stopped, shocked, as the dog bounded out of the cab and shot across the road into a row of shrubbery.

Scott tracked his new friend into the bushes and knelt down to pat his head. "Why did you do that?" he asked in a quiet voice.

The dog merely wagged his tail; tongue hanging out, as if pleased.

Together, they watched the workmen move pieces of furniture out of the van and carry them into the house. Soon, someone shut the van's back door, the movers crowded back into the cab, and they drove away.

A stocky, grubby-looking guy strolled out of the house, emptied the mailbox, picked up the newspapers, and returned, slamming the door behind him.

The dog trotted back to his place on the landing and sniffed at his empty pan. Abruptly, the front door opened again, scaring him off.

The grubby-looking fellow stuck his head out. "What's this?!" He yelled something back to someone inside, snatched up the food pan, and slung it after the fleeing dog. Stomping back inside, he slammed the door behind him.

Scott got to his feet and stepped from the shrubbery. He felt like taking a rock and heaving it through the guy's window. *How can people be so cruel?* He retrieved the food pan from the bushes and ran to the rear of his grandmother's house with the dog close behind.

"Stay." He held his hand out in front of him. With the pan in hand, he slipped through the back door into the kitchen where a mixture of delicious smells still filled the room.

Ralston, busy cleaning off a counter, turned with a scowl frozen on his face, but his eyes soften as he caught sight of the empty pan that Scott held out in front of him. "What do you have?" he asked.

Scott pointed at the back door.

Ralston opened the door to the dog, sitting patiently, waiting.

"No animal should go hungry," Ralston said, taking the pan from Scott and opening the refrigerator door. He returned it, filled with potatoes and a small piece of meat left over from the previous night's dinner. "Now leave before you get my kitchen dirty."

Scott ignored the harsh response. Ralston wasn't nearly as mean as he pretended.

Outside, Scott showed the food to his friend. "Come!" He patted his leg and moved to the side of the house, out of sight from the back door. The dog thumped his tail in appreciation.

Leaving him to eat in peace, Scott returned to the kitchen and walked up behind Ralston as he put a dish on a shelf, tapping him on the shoulder.

Ralston closed the cupboard door and turned to address Scott, "Now what?"

Without thinking, Scott signed like he did with his dad, asking what Ralston knew about the dog.

"Don't understand," he said, shaking his head back and forth.

"The dog," said Scott out loud and pointed at the door.

"You're asking about him?"

Scott nodded.

"Jonesy, his owner, was a truck driver. He called him 'Runt.' The dog went with him everywhere until Jonesy got sick. After he died, his wife sold the house and left, leaving the dog to fend for himself."

That was a lot of words, but Ralston spoke slowly enough that Scott could follow most of it. He now understood. Runt had jumped into the truck hoping to find Jonesy.

Scott placed his hand on his mouth. With a downward gesture, he said, "Thanks."

He continued through the kitchen to the study where he found his dad, reading by the fireplace. He ran up to him and signed, "The dog has no one. May I keep him?"

"Whoa!" his dad exclaimed, putting down his book. "You remember what I told you about your grandmother's allergies?" Before Scott could reply, he added, "Besides, she doesn't like dogs."

Scott gave him his most pleading look and, motioning with a hand, said softly, "I'll keep him away from her."

His dad thought about it, rubbing his chin. "I will be gone a lot, and you do need a friend." He slapped his leg, saying, "All right, the dog doesn't have any tags, so we'll get him a license and a rabies shot. I'll explain to your grandmother. Then, I'll get Ralston to add dog food to the grocery list. He will be your responsibility. You must take care of him. And, as you promised, keep him away from her."

Again, that was a lot of words, but Scott understood that his dad approved as long as he vowed to care for him. He signed, 'I promise,' grinning from ear to ear.

★ ★ ★

Later in the day, there was nobody at home but Ralston, so Scott sneaked Runt upstairs to his room. He had promised to keep Runt away from The Ark, but nothing was said about keeping him out of his room. Together, they lay on the floor in front of the television. His dad had brought Scott's TV up from the car. It had a special device for watching captioned programs. Unfortunately, there existed only one station that provided caption service.

They were wrestling on the floor during a commercial when Ralston looked in. Scott cringed, expecting to be fussed at for bringing the dog upstairs, but Ralston only shook his head, rolled his eyes, and left.

That evening after supper, Scott took Runt's food dish to the side of the house next to the water pail. He filled it with dog food and sat nearby to watch him eat. No one was around to tease him about his voice if it should crack, so he leaned against the side of the house and spoke in a half-whisper.

"Runt, I need your help."

Runt kept eating but did turn an ear in Scott's direction.

"I know giving advice is not your strong point," began Scott, "but Sunday is Father's Day. The TV shows golf clubs for sale, also shoes, and shirts, but I don't have enough money. Besides, I don't think Dad plays golf."

Runt's tail hit the side of the house with a steady, rhythmic beat. Scott could feel the vibrations.

"I take it you agree."

Runt raised his head a moment before dropping his head into the water pail.

"I know, I know," Scott replied to an imaginary response. "It's the thought that counts. But for this Father's Day, I want to do more than draw him a picture." He dug deep into his pockets and pulled out a couple of dollar bills along with a handful of coins. "Maybe I can get him a store-bought card. Tomorrow, we'll go to the store."

After a slurp of water from the water pail, Runt suddenly turned and gave him a sloppy kiss across the face.

"Yuck!" Scott hopped to his feet. "Don't get me wrong, but I could have done without that." He patted Runt and gave him a goodnight hug before heading back inside.

Chapter 4

Abandoned Again

When Scott came down the next morning, he found Ralston waiting for him at the bottom of the stairs. "Your dad went to Wichita. He won't be back until this afternoon."

Scott moved his hand from his mouth and down to say 'thanks,' then reached for the door that led into the breakfast room.

Before he could open it, he felt the housekeeper's hand on his shoulder. "He left this for you." Ralston handed him a small, metal tag and a signed library application.

Scott studied them for a moment.

"Attach the tag to Runt's collar," Ralston said, "and if you take this application to the library, they will issue you a card to check out books."

"Thanks."

Ralston forewarned, "Your grandmother is already at the table."

Instant anxiety. He never knew what to expect from her.

The Ark sat at the breakfast table. While holding a cup of coffee in one hand, she held the newspaper with the other. She appeared to study it as if it were a novel of great interest.

"Good morning," Scott said softly, hoping his voice was under control.

His grandmother acknowledged with a cut of her eyes and continued reading while Ralston brought Scott some juice and biscuits. Shortly, The Ark put down her cup and dropped the paper back on the table. She waved a hand at him as if attempting to communicate with a household pet. After enunciating the word, "Good-bye," she spoke with Ralston, uttering instructions before leaving.

Scott knew his grandmother had her own friends and activities and no time for a deaf grandson with whom she had nothing in common.

Getting up from the table, Scott kicked the chair back into place. *Why did Dad go off and leave me with such a person?* He slammed the door behind him as he went outside to call for Runt. Attaching the dog license to his collar, he said, "Come on, Runt, let's go."

Runt wagged his tail with enthusiasm and accompanied Scott to the library and waited by the door.

Scott checked out a paperback about gymnastics, then

headed to the small park where he and Runt had first become friends. He stopped at the base of a stout Elm. "Wait," he commanded. "Don't worry. I'll be back. I just want to go where I won't be bothered for a while."

Leaving Runt at the base of the tree, he put the paperback under his belt and climbed up the trunk, bracing himself comfortably in a fork of the branches.

Gazing across the nearby open field, he thought Kansas might not be such a bad place to live. It was a beautiful day, and everything was peaceful. Below, Runt had curled up by the tree's roots.

Opening his book, Scott turned to a page with the caption, A NATIONAL MEET. On the top half of it was a photo taken of the interior of a gymnasium filled with observers and competitors.

With longing in his heart, he shut his eyes, remembering the last time he competed with his team in Texas…

They arrived at the gym and began their stretching exercises. After a few minutes, they lined up with the other teams facing the spectators. An announcer introduced each team, and then everyone stood for the National Anthem.

His first event was the pommel horse. At the chalking station, he dusted his hands to keep from slipping on the apparatus, then moved to the horse and waited for his coach who gave him an encouraging thumbs up.

Scott raised a thumb in response. Facing the judges, he

waited patiently for them to look up, so he could signal he was ready.

The head judge did, and Scott raised his arm...

Scott felt something hit his face. Startled, his eyes flew open. A small twig with a couple of leaves on it lay in his lap. He looked above and saw a pair of brown squirrels chasing each other through the limbs.

He closed his eyes again, thinking, *The Ark thinks I'm deaf and dumb. Well, I'll show her just how dumb I am. So what if Mom is in Heaven and Dad leaves at the drop of a hat? I will succeed despite them all.* Gymnastics was his thing. It was his way of showing the world that he existed; that he was really there.

...Again, he remembered the tension and excitement he felt that day as he placed his hands on the pommel. Mounting it, he swung both legs in a circular motion above it. He performed across the entire length of the horse, culminating with a handstand and dismount. "Yes!" he exclaimed, raising his fist...

Suddenly, Scott felt himself falling. He flailed his arms about as he opened his eyes, realizing where he was. Clutching the tree trunk, his book disappeared through the branches. He half-slid, half-climbed, back to the base of the tree.

As Runt jumped about, he picked himself off the ground. "Calm down. I'm all right."

After brushing some of the bark off his clothes and grabbing his book, he headed for the stream to wash off the dirt. The cool water stung his scrapes. He hissed as he rubbed the dirt from his wounds. *In the future, I'm reading and daydreaming in a safer place. Ouch!*

Returning to his grandmother's house, he found a couple of Band-Aids under the bathroom sink.

"Interesting," said Ralston. Watching him doctor a skinned place, he tapped Scott's shoulder. "How did you do that?"

"Fell out of a tree," he replied in a half-whisper as he used a 'V' shape to illustrate.

"Hmm… Are you hungry?"

"Yes." After being presented with a sandwich, a cookie, and a glass of milk, he signed 'thanks.'

Ralston replied, smiling, "You're welcome."

Scott took part of his sandwich outside and fed it to Runt. They left for the stream that snaked its way through the middle of town. Following it past the city limits, they moved on to the river.

The river flowed gently in several places over shallow stones. In one place, it formed a deeper pool at the base of a series of solid, white boulders. The ground was so soft that Scott's foot plunged into it, causing him to trip and fall into the water. Runt jumped in behind him, grabbed the seat of his shorts, and tugged him toward the shore.

Scott laughed. Though humorous, it was also annoying. "Hey, Runt, let go! I'm fine." But he persisted until Scott climbed all the way back onto the bank.

Regardless of Runt's concern, Scott shed his shirt, shoes, and socks, then jumped back in. He was a good swimmer, and it had been a long time since he had played in the water.

At first, Runt just stood on the bank.

"Come, Runt, the water's fine." Scott reached for a stick. He threw it into the middle of the pool. "Fetch!"

Runt hesitated, his head pivoting from Scott to the stick until deciding to take the plunge. He retrieved it and paddled back. The two of them enjoyed playing and splashing until Scott's stomach sounded the dinner alarm.

"Let's go, Runt! It's late!" Scott climbed out, grabbed his shirt, and used it to dry himself off, squeezing his shorts as best he could.

Runt joined him and vigorously shook himself.

"Hey!" Wet all over again, he put on his socks and shoes, tied his wet shirt around his waist, and started home.

The sun had dropped below the horizon when they turned up the street.

Scott stopped dead in his tracks. A police car rested against the curb in front of the house and from every window a light beamed out into the dusk.

Immediately, he thought something had happened to his dad. He rushed forward as Ralston, his dad, and a policeman appeared at the door.

With a sigh of relief, Scott slowed to a walk while Runt

stayed in the shadows.

"Scott!" his dad exclaimed.

Scott stopped in front of him and with exaggerated motions gestured his concern.

"Am *I* all right?" his dad asked sternly. "Do you realize what time it is?"

He shook his head.

"Where's your watch?"

He held his wrist up, so his dad could see that it had stopped.

"How? Never mind. We'll talk about that later. Supper's over. Go get ready for bed."

Scott began signing again; wanted desperately to explain.

"No, I don't want to hear it right now. Go!" His dad turned and spoke to the policeman, apologizing and thanking him for coming.

Head cast down, Scott headed up the staircase. Even Ralston showed his disapproval.

All right, I made a mistake. No harm, except maybe to worry Dad.

That night, his dad lectured him. He seemed shocked to learn that Scott had wandered so far from home and went swimming in the river with only Runt for a companion. "Son, we were worried."

"I'm sorry." Scott rotated a sign for the letter 'A' on his chest, staring at the floor.

Clapping him on the shoulder, his dad lifted Scott's chin and spoke to him directly. "Use your head. People are concerned about you and need to know where you are."

Scott spoke and signed, "I can take care of myself."

His dad sighed and leaned back in his chair. "Look, I'm going to have to be out of town for a while."

Scott touched his forehead. "Why?"

"I have to go to Japan to help negotiate a deal for building airplane parts. It means a lot of money for the company. It's what I do."

Scott was sad. *He'll be gone again for weeks, maybe months. Why couldn't he have a job like most people where we could stay together and be a family?*

Charles gently shook Scott's shoulder and he looked up. "While I'm gone, I expect you to cooperate with Ralston and your grandmother."

Scott agreed.

"There ought to be something left in the fridge. No more stunts like today. Remember, we love you, okay?"

Scott raised an eyebrow. The "we" part of his dad's statement puzzled him. It must have meant to include The Ark, but she hadn't been at the door looking for him when he came home.

After his dad left, he went to the kitchen and made a sandwich, then picked up the bag of dog food and slipped out the back door. After filling Runt's food dish, he perched on a stacked pile of firewood and munched on the sandwich while Runt gulped down his meal.

Scott wondered if The Ark's attitude would be different if he were "normal." Maybe he caused the accident that happened so long ago. *Did I distract Mom so much by arguing or complaining that she drove off a cliff?* He couldn't remember. *Maybe this deafness is my punishment.*

Runt finished his supper and demanded attention.

Scott gave him a goodnight pat and started back to the kitchen with the dog food. As he passed the living room window, he noticed his dad and The Ark arguing. His dad faced away from him, so he could only see one side of the conversation.

"I know what he did was inexcusable," said The Ark, "but, like it or not, he's part of the family."

Scott stepped up on a ledge and peered through the window. *Are they talking about me? Sure, I messed up, but, of course, I'm part of the family.*

"It's time for this nonsense to stop," continued The Ark. "It's been over thirteen years, a long time to hold a grudge."

Whew! At least, they're not talking about me.

He didn't know what his dad replied, but it was violent.

"Look," replied The Ark, "I know he's irresponsible. He's always been that way, but maybe he's changed. The last time I heard from him, he planned to get married. Remember, you were friends once. At least, talk to him. Someday, the boy should meet him."

His dad snapped back with a comment and left the room. Scott dropped to the ground. He couldn't imagine what would make his dad so angry. He quietly opened the back door and slipped in. Closing it gently behind him, he went back up the stairs to his bedroom. After cleaning up and brushing his teeth, he put on his pajamas and crawled into bed.

The Ark said, "the boy." That would have to be me. So, who is this person that I should meet? It was late when he finally drifted into a restless sleep.

During the night, a touch half-awakened him. He still remembered how his mother used to come into his room late at night. He would be barely conscious of her when she kissed him on the forehead and tucked the blanket around him.

"Love you, Mom," Scott muttered, crossing his fists across his chest. He sniffed the air. It wasn't perfume but the delicate odor of his dad's aftershave that lulled him into a deeper sleep.

Rustie

His dad had gone.

Scott would have known it even if he hadn't been told it would happen. It was a sort of sixth sense; something he felt in the stillness of the morning.

He yawned, sat up, and swung his feet to the floor. Across the room on his dresser lay a small object that hadn't been there before. Puzzled, he shuffled to it and picked up a sleek, new whittler knife. A note lay underneath it.

Here's something that will help you whittle away your time. If you run into a problem, go to Ralston. I'll have you in my thoughts and prayers.

Be back soon.

Love,

Dad

Scott picked up the knife, sat on the edge of his bed, and opened the blades. It was a marvelous tool, sharp enough to carve into the hardest of woods.

He thought about his dream. His mother had visited him during the night and she had been wearing a perfume that smelled like his dad's aftershave. He looked back at the scrap of paper left on the dresser. It was funny how a person's dream could trick him like that.

It's Sunday! Father's Day! He ran over to his chest of drawers and opened the top one. The card that he had so carefully selected at the store still lay on his socks and underwear. Only, there was no father to receive it. Seven years before, there had been no father to rescue him. That burning inferno had taken his mother's life.

He clenched his fists. His mom was gone, his dad had left. Again, he had been abandoned. Why couldn't he have a home like everyone else? His friends had someone to ask them how their day went. Their parents would come to watch and support them at gym meets. His dad had only shown up once.

The tension inside of him built until his whole body shook. He snatched the card out of the drawer, tore it in half, and threw it in the trash can. Grabbing a chair, he gripped the arms of it so tightly that his knuckles turned white.

This is no good! I have to calm down. Remembering what he had learned long ago, he concentrated on a mental picture.

A swift-moving mountain stream flowed through the midst of a large, green valley. It was surrounded by tall pines and imposing mountains. Here he could relax and let his emotions be swept downstream by the rapid-flowing water. It was one bit of training he never forgot, yet he couldn't remember who had taught it to him.

Finally, feeling in control, he got dressed and headed down the stairs.

Ralston sat at a table in the kitchen with a bowl of cereal, a glass of juice, and a newspaper.

Scott tapped him on the shoulder.

Startled, Ralston dropped the paper. His shocked expression changed back into its customary deadpan look as he asked, "Would you like some breakfast?"

"Yes," Scott said, motioning with his fist.

"How about cereal and juice?"

"Great!"

Ralston started to get up, but Scott motioned him to stay. He walked to the cupboard to find his own bowl and cereal, poured his juice, and pulled up a chair to join the old man at the kitchen table.

Carefully, he spoke. "You knew my dad as a boy?"

"I sure did. Been here a long time."

"He lived here?"

"Yes."

"With Grandmother?"

Ralston's face did not change, but his eyes relaxed a little. "Life changes with time."

Scott thought about that. "Grandmother was different when my dad was a boy?"

"Some."

"What happened?"

"She was a model. She met your grandfather. They were married." Ralston paused. "She had great hopes for the future. That's when your dad was born."

Scott studied Ralston's face. He'd spoken distinctly; had considered every word. "Go on."

"Soon your uncle was born. Then your grandfather became very sick."

Surprised, Scott asked, "I have an uncle?"

"We haven't seen him in many years," said Ralston, sadly.

"So, Grandmother took care of Grandfather and both boys," finished Scott.

"Your grandfather was sick a long time. Your grandmother gave up her work to care for him."

Scott hoped Ralston wouldn't think him weird that it pleased him to understand every word. "Didn't she *have* to work?"

"Your grandfather had money."

Scott thought about what he had learned. If he had to spend years taking care of a sick person, he might be grouchy, too.

"Your grandfather died," continued Ralston. "Your dad left to begin his own life. This left your grandmother to become lonely and bitter."

Scott tried to decipher each word coming from Ralston's lips. The explanations were getting longer, but he'd understood enough. It was wrong to make others unhappy because you are unhappy. It was hard to think of The Ark as being anything but what she was.

"Thanks." He picked up his dishes and carried them to the sink. After signing a goodbye, he headed out the door.

Scott hunted up Runt and they scampered to the stream that ran through the middle of town. On the other side of the stream was a church with a bell tower. Families in their Sunday best were getting out of cars and moving toward the church's entrance. That meant the bell was ringing to signal that a service was about to begin.

He sat on the bank to watch, tossing in a stone. *Maybe I should go to church, too. When Dad's in town on Sunday, we go. Maybe if I went and asked, God would forgive me for causing Mom's death and would give me back my hearing. Then maybe Dad could get a "normal" job and a home we can call ours.*

A tightness built up in the pit of his stomach that wouldn't go away as Scott considered entering the church with all those strangers. *Some other time. Besides, it might not make any difference anyway. Dad claimed the accident wasn't anybody's fault, but he hadn't been there. How would he know?*

A small piece of juniper had washed up on the bank. Scott picked it up, pulled out his new knife, and began to whittle. The wood had broken off from a nearby cedar. It had a sweet-smelling odor with layers of soft colors.

On the trail above, a pair of boys approached in his direction, fishing poles in hand. Scott slapped his thigh to call Runt and moved lower on the bank where he could stay out of sight. The boys passed, never looking in his direction. Watching them walk away, one boy wore a team shirt that was the same color as a gymnastics shirt hanging in his closet.

In Texas, the competitive season would be over. The gym team would be relaxing and having fun. The coach would take them to a swimming pool after workouts. There, they would shock the lifeguard by doing all kinds of daring acrobatics off the diving board.

Scott patted Runt's black and tan coat. *At least I have one friend.* Hopping to his feet, he pocketed the knife and left. He pushed his way through the brush to the trail. Runt trotted along behind, detouring occasionally to chase a rabbit or investigate a smell.

They approached a highway, where a service station was located on the other side. A raised car rested on a rack in the garage, but no one was in sight.

He felt the coins in his pocket. *There should be a drink machine in the office.* With a bit of luck, he could walk in, use the machine, and get out without meeting anyone. He and Runt crossed the road.

As he jogged past the garage door, the smells of a typical garage were all there, yet the odor wasn't unpleasant. A glance inside revealed a redheaded girl with a tough-looking guy near the back of the garage.

Scott moved to the office door. The drink machine was in plain sight on the other side of the room. Entering quietly, he dropped in his money, pulled out a canned drink, and popped the tab. But before he could take a swallow, the can was knocked out of his hands and he was shoved against the counter.

Standing before him was the tough-looking guy from the garage. He jerked the redheaded girl in front of him and pointed at him. "What's wrong with you? You think I'm kidding? I said, *'Back up!'*"

Shocked, Scott scrambled back into a corner.

The man pushed the girl into the corner with him. He opened the register, snatched a handful of bills, and stuffed them into his pocket. Slamming the drawer shut, he spun about to leave. There, he stopped like he had bounced into a pane of glass.

Outside stood Runt; his lip curled back as ferocious as any German shepherd could be. The startled robber turned and ran down the drive with Runt within inches of his rear end, snapping at his heels. They disappeared around the corner of the building.

Scott could see the girl had covered her face; body

trembling, sobbing uncontrollably. He put his hand on her shoulder.

"I'm all right," she said, wiping her eyes with the back of her forearm. She gave him a quick smile.

Satisfied she was okay, he dashed out the door after Runt, hoping he wouldn't be hurt or killed by the robber.

Reaching the corner of the building, Runt reappeared; trotted up to Scott as if he had just been out for a little exercise.

Scott knelt next to him and gave him a hug. "Good boy, Runt. Good boy."

A bit of gravel struck his leg from behind. He pivoted, ready to defend himself. "That's Runt," said the girl. "He used to belong to Horace."

From habit, Scott responded by touching his forehead to say I know.

Confusion cast over her face; eyebrows up and scrunched.

Scott realized she did not understand, so he got to his feet, waved good-bye, and started moving away.

The girl grabbed his arm as he passed by. "Don't go," she pleaded. "I know about you. You're that new kid the guys were talking about. You—You're deaf, aren't you?"

Scott, with his first two fingers, pointed to his eyes and said, "I read much of what you say."

"That's why you didn't stop when I yelled, and why you didn't hear that crook tell you to—Oh, wow!" The girl looked at him as if he had turned into an alien from another world.

Having not actually taken the time to look at the girl, it was then he noticed the sun shone upon her hair, giving it a light, golden tinge. She was pretty in spite of all the freckles. Her tomboyish blue jeans and long-sleeved shirt appeared to be hand-me-downs from an older brother.

Suddenly, a look of alarm crossed the girl's face. "My dad!" she exclaimed. She took off at lightning speed for the garage with Scott in hot pursuit.

Finding her father bound and gagged in a utility closet, the girl removed the filthy cloth from his mouth as Scott untied his hands. Her words tumbled over one another as she explained what had happened; how Runt had chased off the robber.

Raising his hand like a stop sign, her father said, "Hey, calm down! Are you all right?"

"Yes, I think so. I am just shaking a little."

"He didn't hurt you or anything?"

"I'm all right."

"Thank God!" He gave her a hug, waved thanks to Scott, and reached for his cell phone.

The girl breathed a sigh of relief and leaned against the doorframe. "What's your name?"

"Scott."

"Sorry for staring. It's just that I thought deaf people

didn't talk."

"Don't much," he replied in a half-whisper. "Voice sounds funny sometimes."

Runt sat next to him, taking in every nuance of the situation.

"Your voice is fine. I'm Roberta. Roberta McAtee, but most of my friends just call me Rustie." She giggled. "It's spelled with an 'ie.'"

He repeated it quietly, "Rus-tee," expecting her to be shocked with the sound of his voice. Getting none, he was relieved.

"Runt's a great dog, you know." Rustie reached to pet him.

He signed by flipping a finger from his chin, saying, "Tell me."

Rustie crouched to pet Runt and started talking. Scott couldn't see what she said and nudged her, so she would look at him.

"Oh," said Rustie, getting the cue. "Sorry. What I said was, that Horace raised him from a pup. He named him Runt because he was the smallest. Runt rode with him in the rig and learned to drink coffee. He even won a medal for saving a kid's life. He shoved the boy out of the way of a truck." She gave Runt an extra hug and added, "But I don't think he ever chased a robber before."

Speaking a bit too fast, Rustie nevertheless tried to

enunciate, even though he didn't catch all the words.

Rustie patted him on the head and fingered the worn, leather collar about his neck. "Hey, Runt, you need a new collar. We can do something about that. Wait right here."

She disappeared into the back of the building. In a moment, she reappeared, waving a collar; a fine piece of crafted leather with diamond-shaped pieces of turquoise evenly spaced along its length. "See, it's special, for a very special dog."

Scott took off Runt's old collar and attached the license to the new one. He pivoted his finger. "Where?" he asked.

"Where'd it come from?" Rustie understood. "It used to belong to Gizmo, my aunt's golden retriever."

Runt stood patiently while Rustie took the collar and placed it around the dog's neck. "See, it just fits."

Scott beamed.

"Hey!" Rustie exclaimed. "Let me buy you that drink you didn't finish."

He patted his pocket to show he had money.

"Aw, c'mon, I'm just trying to say 'thanks.'"

Scott hesitated but then agreed, signing 'okay.'

Chapter 6

The Rescue

Almost two weeks after the service station robbery, the police caught the robber in another county attempting to hold up a convenience store. Mr. McAtee left for the courthouse to identify him in a lineup while Rustie and her mother were left to run the station.

Scott had become a frequent visitor. On this particular day, he sat on a concrete abutment outside the office, pondering the building storm clouds, and knew that soon he would have to move inside.

Pulling out his knife, he bent over for a branch of elm he'd brought from the river banks, wishing it was from the heart of a May tree. Then he could carve a walking stick that would last a lifetime. The knife reminded him of his dad and he wondered how things were going over in Japan.

Just then, a brilliant flash of light lit up the entire area and, within seconds, a strong vibration followed, which made Scott think of an earthquake. Of course, he knew it was only thunder.

Runt shook all over as if someone had threatened him with a whip.

Scott consoled him, rubbing his head. "It's all right. It's just Nature fussing at us."

Runt showed his appreciation by nudging his hand.

The wind picked up and large drops of rain fell on Scott's shoulders. He grabbed his stick and backed into the doorway of the office. There, he took an empty trash can and turned it upside down to sit on.

Mrs. McAtee approached from behind. He could tell it was her without looking. She had been working on a car and the greasy odor from her overalls preceded her. He turned and waved at her as she gave him a thumbs-up gesture.

Suddenly, someone poked him in the ribs and he jerked around. There was Rustie. "That lightning was awesome and that blast of thunder—! But you didn't hear it, did you?"

He moved the tip of a middle finger up his chest, saying, "I felt it."

"Cool!"

The lightning flashed once more and again Scott felt the vibrations of the thunder. As the rain came down in torrents, he stopped carving to watch small, white chunks of ice bounce on the driveway and in the grass.

Rustie spoke the word, "Hail," which looked like a swear word to him, but he knew what she meant.

Less frequently came the lightning and thunder, leaving a cloudy, dreary day, as the rain continued falling lightly. Scott appreciated the shelter of the office. Soon, a stronger and more regular, throbbing beat was felt.

Puzzled, Scott glanced around and saw Rustie diddy-bopping behind the counter with a bounce, her head moving up and down in a pulsating manner.

For a moment, Scott couldn't understand why she acted so weird. Then he noticed the dial light on the radio and realized it was the music. He got up and placed his hand on the counter where he could feel the sensations.

Rustie poked him and pointed to a large semi pulling up in front of the station.

Scott followed her gaze, then looked back for an explanation.

"Must be in trouble," she said. "They don't usually stop here."

The driver got out, checked his brake lines, and walked into the station's garage.

Scott shrugged and went back to his whittling. It would get dark early because of the clouds and he wanted to finish the top knob on his walking stick. Rustie went back to stocking peanuts and candies on the shelves behind the register.

A moment later, Scott looked up to see the driver wave as he climbed back into his truck. Scott waved back, closed his knife, and dropped it into his pocket, then looked for Runt and slapped his thigh.

No dog.

Scott repeated the action several times. He leaned the stick against the wall and ran out into the drizzling rain. After circling the service station, calling for him, he stopped and searched the whole area.

No trace of the dog.

Frantic, Scott returned to the office door. He rushed inside to find Rustie. Flipping his thumb from under his chin, he shouted, "Runt is not here!"

Rustie stuck her head into the garage. "Mom, have you seen Runt?"

Mrs. McAtee looked up from under the hood of an old Chevy. "Are you kidding? I hardly have time for dog-sitting." Seeing the serious expression on Scott's face, she somberly commented, "You said he likes trucks. Maybe he went to visit the one out front."

Scott scurried back to the door in time to see the long semi pulling out onto the service road. He raced after it as the driver moved into a westbound lane of traffic.

Breathing hard, Scott stopped; the rig gaining speed away from him. The rain fell steadily on his head and shoulders. He shivered a little, but barely noticed it. A tight feeling knotted in his stomach, recalling Runt's dog tag. That pup couldn't resist trucks, especially rigs, and Scott felt certain he could be nowhere else.

After a tap on his shoulder, he spun about. Rustie stood behind him with an old plastic bin lid over her head, pointing at the nearest field. "Maybe he ran after a rabbit."

Scott shook his head 'no.' Runt might chase after something, but he wouldn't be gone this long.

His heart ached. To him, Runt was more than just a friend. Scott could talk to him and Runt would listen, not ignore him. Without him, Scott felt very much alone.

Rustie grabbed his arm and pulled him back into the office. Leaving Scott to gawk at the empty highway, she stepped into the garage to talk with her mother. Soon, she returned and nudged him. "Jonesy had a terrible time keeping Runt out of his rig. He would hop in it every chance he got. That driver said he would stop at Annie's Truck Stop and get his brakes checked. It's about quitting time. We can drive there when Mom closes."

Scott regarded Rustie's bike through the window, leaning against the wall, then asked her with his eyes.

Rustie's mouth dropped open in recognition. "No, Scott!" she exclaimed. "You can't. It's too dangerous."

Scott touched his thumb to his chest. "I'm fine." He ran out to the bike, hopped on, and took off; never once looking back as he pedaled into the access lane. He knew Rustie would

be yelling and running after him. Fortunately, the highway wasn't busy, and a paved shoulder lay next to the roadway.

The flat, almost treeless, landscape extended to the horizon. Nevertheless, there were times he had to pump up a long, gradual incline.

A misty drizzle assailed him, making his trek even more miserable. Bridges were a special challenge. Because of them, the shoulder disappeared. That meant he had to look behind him for oncoming traffic.

At almost dusk, he detected the odor of hamburgers. Pedaling hard to top a hill, the truck stop came into view. The huge parking area held all sizes and kinds of rigs. He stopped on the shoulder near a bridge and caught his breath while studying the license plates.

He saw the rig he wanted, moving from the parking lot onto an on-ramp. Hopping back on the bike, he pumped forward into the outside lane of traffic. He felt a rumble. A car had slipped sideways on the damp pavement behind him. Waving an apology, he continued. With every ounce of strength, he passed in front of the truck's headlights, as it headed for the entrance to the highway. He could smell the heat from the engine and felt the screech of the truck's brakes. His bike slipped off the pavement and headed into a ditch.

The trucker swung down from the cab. Runt jumped down behind him and dashed to the ditch where Scott had fallen.

A pickup pulled up. Rustie bolted out of it.

Scott saw the truck's headlights and realized that for the second time, in as many minutes, he had almost been hit by a vehicle. But everything was all right now. He sat in the mud and threw his arms around Runt who licked him nonstop on the face.

The trucker, very upset at almost killing a kid on a bike, looked from boy to dog to girl, then demanded, "What's this all about?"

Rustie started to explain, but her mother rushed up and interrupted. She told the driver what happened.

Grabbing Scott by the arm, Rustie crouched in front of him where he could see her face reflected in the headlights of the rig. "You idiot! What were you thinking? You could've gotten killed. I talked Mom into closing early and coming after you. You're lucky the cops didn't pick you up. Don't you know it's against the law to ride a bike on the interstate?"

Scott wiped the rain off his face. He understood much of what she said. *So what? Runt was a lot more important than any old law.* He gave his pal another big hug.

The driver explained, "Runt and me, we've been friends for a long time. Jonesy teamed up with me for a few long runs, and the dog went with us. We became good friends.

"Look," the driver addressed Mrs. McAtee, "I'm sorry if I upset the kid and made him think I was stealing his dog.

I would've brought him back on my return trip. Runt just sat there, begging, so when I got in the rig, us being good friends and all, I just sort of let him come along."

Rustie tugged on Scott. "C'mon, let's get the bike into the back of the pickup. Your grandmother will probably be looking for you."

Scott gave Runt a final hug and got to his feet. He didn't argue but doubted that The Ark would care one way or another about him. Runt shook off his coat, and then hopped into the cab of the pickup as they loaded the bike.

The rain had stopped by the time Mrs. McAtee pulled up in front of Scott's grandmother's house. The porch light switched on. Scott knew he looked a mess, but he didn't care. As Runt ran to hide in the shadows, Rustie and Mrs. McAtee walked with Scott to the door, greeted Ralston, and explained what happened.

The Ark came to the door in a huff. Scott could see she was *not* happy. She acted polite but blunt. She took one look at Scott and motioned him up the stairs with her thumb.

Entering past Ralston, Scott signed 'good-bye' to Rustie and two-stepped to the top landing, then stopped. There, he turned and watched. His grandmother faced away from him, but he could see Mrs. McAtee's reaction to The Ark's comments.

"I agree," said Mrs. McAtee, "Scott didn't use good judgment. But still, he is very talented, especially when you consider his handicap. You must be proud of his athletic ability. Not many deaf boys are that capable, you know."

The Ark's reply was brief and not very enthusiastic, then Rustie and her mom sadly retreated to their truck. Afterward, she said something to Ralston about how 'that did it and she would call someone.'

Scott analyzed those words on his way to the bathroom to clean up and get ready for bed. He thought about Mrs. McAtee's comments. She had described him as a good athlete for a deaf boy. He couldn't help feeling some resentment. *Why did people believe that kids who weren't deaf should be better at doing stuff than those that were?*

He hadn't had any supper, but it did not matter. *Not hungry anyway. Besides, I can always raid the refrigerator later. Oh, no! Will The Ark call Dad?*

He thought about his mother. *If she was here, she would come by my room and let me apologize for causing her to worry. The Ark didn't look worried, only angry. Is Dad going to be mad? Maybe he'll come home.*

Scott pounded his pillow. *How stupid! Dad is on the other side of the world and doesn't have time to worry about a deaf son.*

Fury built inside, so he tried to focus on the stream and mountains that would calm him. This time it wasn't working. The images became blurred, then disappeared completely.

His mother's picture sat on the dresser. Scott studied every nuance. The accident that took her life should never have happened. His stomach tripled into a knot again. This time, it made him gasp for air as his whole body shook. He picked up a pillow and threw it, knocking the picture to the floor. Then he sprawled facedown across his bed and sobbed until a restless sleep overtook him.

Fourth of July

The Fourth of July started in a kaleidoscope of color as the first rays of light produced a world bathed in the golden hues of a rising sun. Streaks of clouds caused splinters of fire to stretch along the horizon.

Scott opened the window and sat on the edge of his bed. The cool, early morning air carried the fragrance of wildflowers and roses. He studied the colorful scene as the hues softened; the sun climbing higher in the sky.

Observing a sparrow sitting in the branches of a sycamore tree outside his window, he thought, *Does its movements mean the bird was chirping, singing, or just breathing hard?*

He quickly dressed and ran downstairs to the dining room. The Ark wasn't up yet, so he joined Ralston in the kitchen for breakfast. After a glass of milk and a piece of toast, he told him he was going to visit Rustie and dashed out the door. Runt met him at the bottom of the porch steps and they sauntered in the direction of the park.

It was a pleasant morning, one of those days when everything seemed right with the world. The sun shone brightly, and a flurry of vibrant butterflies filled the air.

Approaching a stout, wooden fence, Scott hopped up on the railing, balancing himself with the air of a tight rope performer. He remembered a trick he used to do and flipped into a handstand. With legs outstretched, he kept his balance while walking on his hands along the rail. Reaching the gate, which presented too great an obstacle, he flipped back to the sidewalk.

At the park, he approached the base of an old Sycamore; the temptation too great. In spite of his last tree-climbing disaster, he motioned Runt to stay while he flitted from branch to branch, to the highest crotch in the tree. There he perched, mesmerized by the expanse of the horizon.

Across the highway, a tractor plowed through a field; the smell of fresh, overturned earth drifted over him. Scott soon looked to the skyline. Somewhere, literally on the other side of the world, his dad talked with the Japanese while volcanoes erupted, and people ate sushi. Someday, he might do the same; go to meet people who were different and see unusual sights.

Knowing it still didn't work, he checked his watch

anyway, then decided to move on. Maybe he, Rustie, and Runt could do something together. Runt raced by his side while he did a series of back flips across the baseball diamond.

After cutting through the woods, Scott plodded up the service station's drive. Rustie stepped out to meet him as Runt trotted up to nuzzle her hand.

Rustie laughed and patted Runt. "We'd better stay away from trucks, little buddy."

Scott agreed wholeheartedly.

"What you did last time, Scott, really freaked me out. It was pretty awesome, but it sure was dangerous."

Scott didn't appreciate being reminded about it. A touch brought his eyes back to her. She grabbed his hand and placed in it a small whistle attached to a rolled-up lanyard.

"Mom got it for you!" she announced. "It's for dogs. Runt will know when you're looking for him."

Scott placed the lanyard about his neck and blew on the whistle.

Runt instantly picked up his ears and looked at him.

"See," said Rustie, "it works." She pointed at her ears. "I can't hear it, but Runt can."

Scott touched his lips and dropped his hand. "Thanks!"

"It's the Fourth of July! There's a parade this morning. Let's go watch it." Rustie hiked her thumb towards town.

"Cool!" he said.

Side by side, with their trusted companion, they headed

to the town center and the best place they could find to view the festivities.

Upon their return, they offered to help Rustie's dad change oil in an old Buick and patch a tire while Rustie talked excitedly about the parade.

"It was awesome," she said. "The band from our high school sounded the best."

"Oh, yeah!" exclaimed Scott, touching his head and pointing at her.

Both Rustie and her father were befuddled.

He looked from one to the other, spread his hands, and asked, "What? Did my voice sound bad?"

"No, silly," said Rustie. "We are wondering how you knew how the band sounded."

"I felt the drums, and they marched together. They also had straight lines. They had to be the best."

Rustie swiveled her head back and forth. "Scott, it might not always work like that."

He touched his forehead and brought his hand down into a 'Y' as he asked, "Why?"

"Because—"

Rustie's father answered the phone and motioned at Scott, interrupting her explanation, "Ralston says it's almost time for supper, and your grandmother wants you home *right now.*"

Scott gave him a thumbs-up. The Ark was probably angry when she found out he had gone. He went into the service station office where Mrs. McAtee worked and tapped her shoulder.

"Thanks. Thanks for the whistle," he said softly.

"You're welcome. Just see that you keep track of Runt. Don't let him leave with my customers," she joked.

Scott chuckled. Outside, he blew on the whistle to see if it still would get the dog's attention. Again, Runt picked up his ears and came right to him.

He waved 'bye' to Rustie.

She waved back and said, "Maybe I'll come by later."

Scott signed 'okay.' Rustie was picking up on some of the simpler signs and he would keep introducing more. He stuck his hands in his pocket and begrudgingly headed down the drive while Runt ran on ahead.

The Ark was waiting for him. When he opened the door, she stepped into the hall. "Your father called," she announced. "Fortunately, Ralston guessed where you were."

"What did he say?" asked Scott, hoping his voice remained under control.

"Not much, only that he would be away longer than planned."

Scott's heart fell in his stomach at the news. On his way to the kitchen, he stopped to look back at her. She was still talking, "...concerned that you had left without permission and suggested you spend the rest of the evening in your room. Incidentally, you are to make up your bed every morning before you do anything else. Is that understood?"

Scott's line of sight went from The Ark to the back-porch screen door. The sun was setting on the horizon. *Dinnertime.* He smelled a ham cooking in the kitchen. *It's plum foolish to make up a bed every morning. I'll just mess it up again.*

He looked back at his grandmother and asked, "Why?"

It felt like she was boring a hole through him with a laser as her face reddened. Scott could imagine smoke coming out of her ears.

She distinctly enunciated each word as she spoke, "*Because -I-said-so.*"

Scott decided there was little to be gained by arguing. Without bothering to sign, he replied, "Yes, Ma'am," and trudged up the stairs.

★ ★ ★

As the sky darkened with the approach of evening, Scott entered the kitchen and pulled out Runt's food sack. The light in the kitchen flicked on, scaring Scott. He expected to find The Ark glaring at him. Instead, Ralston stood in the doorway, branishing a clothes brush above his head.

"It's you!" he exclaimed.

"Yes," said Scott. "I forgot to feed Runt. He had no supper."

"I thought you were a thief."

"Ha!" Scott pointed at the clothes brush, smirking. "Your weapon?"

"It was the only thing handy." Ralston thrust the brush behind his back. "You should be less noisy."

Gripping the dog food sack to his chest, Scott moved to the door. "Sorry, I can't hear myself."

As Ralston turned to leave, he pointed to the switch. "Also, turn off the light."

"Okay." Smiling, he thought about Ralston and the clothes brush. He also felt proud of himself, having understood everything Ralston said.

The day's activities had delayed the normal schedule of things, and as Scott had figured, Runt was hungry. Eagerly, he started devouring the food before Scott could set the bowl on the floor.

Suddenly, the dog froze midbite and stared at the bushes.

A Late Celebration

Someone pushed back the branches and flashed a light in Scott's eyes. Heart racing, he shielded his face and stepped back, searching for a weapon to defend himself. Then the light turned upward into the smiling face of its owner.

"It's just me," announced Rustie, shining the flashlight on Runt, patting him on the head.

"You scared me," said Scott.

Runt wagged his tail. But after sniffing at the plastic bag in Rustie's hand, his tail tucked between his legs and he backed off, wary.

Scott raised an eyebrow and pointed. "What's that?"

Rustie replied something, but he couldn't see what she said in the fading light. He took her flashlight and stuck it under her chin so he could see her lips.

"This is a surprise!" She pulled a Roman candle from the bag. "Jake, the guy at the fireworks stand, gave it to me."

"Why?"

"Guess he likes me," she replied, sheepishly. "Let's go to the park and shoot it off."

"I don't think so. It's late." He shook his head and raised his fist with extended thumb, "Tomorrow."

"No!" she insisted. "Now!"

"It's late," he repeated. *After what happened before with The Ark, I don't want any more issues.*

"But it's the Fourth!" exclaimed Rustie. "It wouldn't be the same. This can be *our* celebration."

She may be right. Today is something to celebrate.

He held out his hands palms up, offering back her flashlight, then set the dog food sack against the building. Runt gulped down the few remaining morsels of food as they walked off, then caught up with them.

At the park, Rustie moved to the pitcher's mound on the baseball diamond.

"Hold Runt!" she commanded. "Long ago, he saw a kid get burned with fireworks. Guess that's why he gets so excited."

Scott backed off to a safe distance, holding Rustie's flashlight with one hand and Runt by the collar with the other.

Runt whined, twisted, and reeled in a frenzy of alarm.

When Rustie struck a match and lit the Roman candle, the dog jerked away from Scott's grasp. He charged the sparkling fuse, knocking the candle on its side, pawing at it. As it continued to sparkle, he snatched the tube between his teeth, shook it, and dropped it.

Scott was frantic with what was happening. "Down!" he yelled.

The two of them flattened out on the ground like a pair of soldiers under attack as the rocket discharged. It shot a streak of fire into the wooded area next to the baseball diamond. Filling the air with the smell of burning powder, the rocket bounced from tree to tree. It split and flared until the entire area was bathed in a flaming glow.

Runt shot across the ball diamond and disappeared into the shadows while the light diminished into a scattering of flames.

From the ground, Scott froze, gaping at a line of blazing shrubbery.

A couple of young people passing nearby rushed in, stomping out small fires.

During the confusion, the silhouette of a man moved toward them with long, quick strides. Scott flashed Rustie's light on him as he crouched in front of them.

Ralston's stern features scowled at them. "Why are you here? Are you trying to burn down the neighborhood?"

"How did you know?" Scott asked.

"Didn't," said Ralston. "I saw the flare when I went in to turn off the kitchen light."

"We—We didn't mean to start a fire," stuttered Rustie. "We were just shooting off a rocket."

"Don't you realize you could have been hurt?"

"It was my idea," admitted Rustie, with a sorrowful look. "I'm sorry. It would have been all right if Runt hadn't charged at it."

"No excuses," said Ralston, shaking his head. "Stupid. It was just plain stupid." Within a second, his features softened. "However, you two aren't the first to pull something like this."

Scott was shocked, though he had already decided that Ralston wasn't as mean as he looked.

Ralston ensured the flames were completely out and left, while Scott walked Rustie back to her house.

Near her porch light, she stopped and said, "Sorry. Guess I got you into trouble."

Scott signed 'okay.' "That's all right."

"I can go back with you to explain to your grandmother it was my fault."

Scott squinched his lips. "With her, it might make things worse."

Quick as a flash, Rustie planted a kiss on his cheek and ran up the porch steps to her front door.

Scott gasped. *What just happened??*

When Scott arrived home, there was The Ark waiting by the door. He had never seen her so furious. Her face was flaming and she was trembling so hard he thought she might have a stroke.

The Ark shouted a lot of things, most of which he couldn't follow. After raving about what the neighbors might think and the embarrassment he had caused, she concluded, "That's it! I will take no more!"

She pointed to the stairs.

Slowly, Scott started up the staircase, each foot cement blocks.

Ralston appeared in the doorway and explained, "It wasn't me. The neighbors complained."

Scott touched his sleeve in appreciation. Rapid thoughts ran through his mind, *Why's The Ark so angry? We just went to the park to shoot off a rocket. Although we did scare the wits out of Runt and set the woods on fire, no real harm was done. What did she mean that she would 'take no more?'*

He smiled as something else came to him. *Maybe she'll call Dad to come and get me.* He kept that vision in a safe place within his heart while he got ready for bed. As he drifted off to sleep, he imagined his dad arriving at the airport and buying another ticket for him before coming to the rescue.

★ ★ ★

Saturday came and passed without incident. Having heard nothing, he became resigned to the fact that nothing was going to change. He remembered a story about a boy named Toby who had run off to join a circus. *But what kind of job would they offer a deaf kid?*

When Ralston woke him on Sunday morning, Scott sat up with a start. No one, other than his dad, had ever come into his bedroom before breakfast. The housekeeper sat on the edge of Scott's bed and spoke carefully. "Mrs. Schroeder asked that I help you pack."

"Pack?" Scott spoke and signed, "Why?"

Ralston said nothing for a moment, just studied Scott's face. "Scott, your uncle lives in California."

"He-he what?" He ran his hands over his face and through his short blonde hair.

"Your grandmother called and made arrangements," continued Ralston. "You will stay with your uncle until your father returns."

"You told me about him," said Scott, "but I have never met him. He may not want me. Maybe I can stay with my aunt in Alaska."

Ralston spoke slowly. "That is not possible. Mrs. Schroeder has arranged differently. Your Uncle Todd wants you to come, although he and your father have not talked in years." He closed his eyes slowly, then opened them. "They were very angry the last time they saw each other."

"Why?"

"They argued over a girl."

Scott realized it had to have been awfully serious to not communicate for that long.

"Dad won't like it."

Ralston held his hand. "When your father and uncle were boys, things were different... But that was then, and this is now."

Scott placed a thumb against his forehead and formed a claw hand as he said, "But won't Dad be angry?"

"Perhaps, but maybe this will make him and his brother talk with each other again."

Scott didn't want to play a part in this reunion. Nevertheless, The Ark had made up her mind and there was little he could do. *What about Rustie?* His heart sank. *She's my best friend!* Back in Texas, the guys on the gymnastics team had also been his friends. It was happening again. Every time he made friends, he left and had to find new ones all over again.

"Runt!" he exclaimed. "Where's Runt?"

"Outside."

"I can't leave him." Scott made a fist and placed a thumb under his chin. "The Ark, she would call the dog catchers."

"The who?" Ralston raised an eyebrow.

"Grandmother! The Ark!" shouted Scott. "Runt, he must go with me."

"Impossible." Ralston snorted. "You can't take a dog to California."

Scott made a fist with both hands. "I can."

"There's no way."

"Then I won't go."

"You must!"

Scott was determined.

Ralston stood up and walked to the window. In a moment, he turned back to Scott. Though his face remained solemn, a defiant twinkle was in his eyes. "All right," he said. "I'll rent a carrier but say *nothing* to your grandmother."

"Deal." He walked over to him, signed 'thanks,' and stuck out his hand.

As Ralston shook hands with him, his face lit up. This was the first time the old man had ever stood up to the old woman.

Uncle Todd

The Ark waited near the door as Scott came down the stairs. "Your uncle will take better care of you than me. Cooperate with him and make your father proud."

He could not believe it. Carefully speaking, he asked, "What if Dad calls?"

"I'll take care of it."

Scott signed 'good-bye' and turned away, without a backwards glance. He thought of his dad and how The Ark was so different.

Again, he was leaving. Again, he was alone, except for Runt. Again, he was going someplace he had never been, to live with someone he had never met. His eyes brimmed with tears.

While Ralston loaded his bags, Scott looked for Runt.

He blew on his whistle. When he bounded up to him, Scott crouched down and petted him. He had given him a water hose bath the day before and he was all shiny. Hugging his pal, he explained, "Well, Runt, we're on the go. And this time, you're going with me."

At the airport, Ralston helped Scott get Runt tagged and settled into his Dog-A-Port. Runt protested as a baggage handler took him away.

While standing in line at the ticket counter, Scott turned to Ralston. "Do you have a picture of Uncle Todd?"

"I am afraid not. Your grandmother destroyed most, if not all of them."

"How will I know him?"

"No problem." The elderly man, whose veins were beginning to shine blue on the back of his hands, crouched down in front of Scott, holding both shoulders, comforting him. "Imagine your father with blonde hair. Also, he has a photo of you and knows a lot about you."

Scott signed and asked, "How?"

"Because I told him." Ralston stood upright and picked up Scott's bag as they shuffled forward in the line. "You're his only nephew."

"Oh."

"You'll like him," insisted Ralston, giving him a knowing look. "He's like your father in many ways."

Scott wondered if that meant he would leave the country

for days on end.

After Ralston got him checked in and was given his boarding pass—having made sure Scott had been registered as Special Needs as well as a minor traveling unaccompanied; that he would be allowed to escort him to the gate and wait with him until boarding—he motioned for Scott to shoulder his knapsack and they headed for the Security Checkpoint, then on to the gate. Scott beelined for the massive window overlooking the tarmac. Handlers scurried around in the tugs, towing carts full of luggage.

Scott knew that pets were well taken care of. Still, he hoped Runt would not be too traumatized. After all, Runt was the only one who didn't run off and abandon him… well, as long as there wasn't a truck around.

Without warning, someone grabbed him from behind. Scott whirled about in time to receive a kiss planted in the center of his forehead.

"Rustie!" Surprised, his ears turned red. "Where? How?"

Rustie laughed, pointing to Ralston. "He called us. You don't think we'd let you get away without saying good-bye, do you?"

Mrs. McAtee, who had arranged with TSA (Transportation Security Administration, who rarely *ever* let anyone past the Security Checkpoints) to surprise Scott, stepped forward and kissed him on the cheek. She still carried the oily odor of a mechanic even though she wore a dress.

"We'll miss you," she said, sniffling.

Scott choked up, too. He crossed both hands over his chest, then pointed to her, signing, "I love you."

Ralston announced that a voice over the speaker had urged passengers to start boarding their flight.

Scott shook hands with him and signed 'thank you,' then hugged the old man firmly, saying, "For everything."

After hugging Rustie and her mother, Scott moved forward in line and waved good-bye. With an airline representative by his side, they scanned his boarding pass and headed down the gangway. Tears filled his eyes as he boarded the plane. She helped him find his place and store his knapsack.

Scott signed 'thanks.'

She then gave him instructions using sign language.

Scott had been through it all before and knew what to do. Flopping into his window seat, he buckled his seat belt and looked out. He didn't want any company and felt fortunate that the aisle seat next to him remained empty.

He wiped a sleeve across his face to clear the tears from his eyes. Staring out the window, he looked at nothing in particular. The way things were, he would not go to school with Rustie in the fall, and he'd been looking forward to that.

He pulled the whistle out from under his shirt, attached to the lanyard around his neck. Rubbing his finger across it, he resolved he would never take it off.

He rehashed what Ralston had told him. *How could a girl be so special that his dad and uncle would be angry for so long? This uncle must be the person Dad and The Ark were talking about on that night I watched them through the window.*

Another thought troubled him. *How am I to communicate with Uncle Todd? Hopefully, he'll be more like Dad than The Ark.* He would have to use his voice and hoped he could control it.

After take-off, Scott became drowsy as the prairie, deserts, and mountains passed below him. He tried to imagine his dad with blonde hair, but the figure became blurred in his mind.

★ ★ ★

Scott, accompanied by an airline representative, stepped from the ramp into the corridor at the Los Angeles terminal. Crowds of people were bustling in every direction. Anxiously, he thought, *What if no one is here to meet me? What do I do? Where would I go?*

Suddenly, he spotted a tall, blonde man waving above the crowd of passengers and greeters. Ralston was right. It was like looking at an image of his dad wearing a blonde wig. There could be no mistake. Yet, there was something else. This man had deep, blue eyes and a younger, wilder, less-disciplined appearance, like an adventurer or an explorer. He looked like someone who wouldn't hesitate to stow away on a spaceship and head for the stars; someone who didn't mind taking risks; someone who might do something dangerous if the goal was worthy.

The man made his way to him through the crowd and held out a hand. "You must be Scott. I'm your Uncle Todd."

Scott grinned broadly, shaking his uncle's hand firmly, then signed 'hello,' and said, "Hi!"

Todd thanked the airline representative, then guided Scott down the corridor to an escalator. "This is the way to the carousel."

Scott's mouth fell open again. *Why would an airport have a care and sell? I don't want them to sell my stuff! And where's Runt! They'd better not sell him!*

Silently, he scolded himself. *Remember what your teacher said. "When something doesn't make sense, put syllables together in your mind and try again." Care and sell, care-n-sell, care-a-sell, carousel. All right! That's more logical, but a carousel is a merry-go-round.* He scratched his head. When traveling with the gymnastics team, he had picked up his stuff at a Baggage Claim. It was amusing that so many words could mean the same thing.

Right now, Runt was the most important thing. Pointing to a sign showing the way to the Baggage Claim Area, Scott said, "Runt, I must find him." He ditched a puzzled-looking uncle behind as he raced down an escalator, dodging between passengers. Finding an airline representative, he showed his receipt for Runt.

The representative read it and pointed to an office door, instructing him to wait there. Soon, another employee arrived, rolling Runt on a dolly, locked in his Dog-A-Port. In his own form of sign language, Runt said, "About time!" The employee asked for a leash, so Scott dug into his knapsack, pulled one out, and snapped it on the dog's collar, then led him out of the cage.

Scott petted Runt to assure him all was well. His uncle walked up with a question all over his face.

"Th-This is Runt," said Scott, somewhat concerned, hoping Ralston had told him about bringing the dog and that his uncle was not like The Ark and disliked dogs.

Todd scratched his head. "What a surprise!" He extended a hand to Runt, who sniffed cautiously. "Looks like a good dog. Smart, independent. I'm surprised your grandmother let you have him. She would never let me or your dad have one."

Yeah, I know. Speaking hesitantly and interlocking his index fingers, he said, "He is my friend."

"I understand." Todd motioned toward the carousel. "Let's get your stuff."

In a few moments, they were on the way through the parking garage loaded down with a pair of bags and Runt on a leash. Scott grabbed his uncle's arm and tugged him in another direction.

"Hey, now!" his uncle said. "Where are we going?"

Scott pointed at a drink machine.

"That I can handle!"

Setting down Scott's bag, he slapped his nephew on the shoulder. "Drinks are on me."

They got a couple of sodas and sat on a concrete block with Scott's bags in front of them. Todd, speaking slowly and distinctly, told him about his partners, Joseph Goens, whom he called Jo-Go, and Jo-Go's wife, Tammie. "We sell gliders and teach folks how to fly them."

Scott rubbed Runt behind the ears and beamed from ear to ear. Flying in a glider sounded exciting and he hoped his uncle would take him up in one. He knew about airplanes. More than once he had flown on a commercial airliner to competitions with the gymnastics team. *Yet, that wouldn't be the same as soaring through the sky in a glider!*

"This is Jo-Go," said Todd, waving at an approaching figure. "I guess he got tired of waiting."

With short, curly, black hair and a broad smile, Jo-Go strode over. Scott got up and held out his hand.

"So, you're Scott." Jo-Go laughed as they shook hands. "My friend, you're a scholar and a gentleman!"

Scott raised an eyebrow. He didn't understand the "scholar" part, but replied with voice and gesture, "Who? Me?"

"Yeah, he's talking about you." Todd chuckled.

"Thanks!" signed Scott. A familiar odor made a picture of Mrs. McAtee flash through his mind. *Jo-Go must also be a mechanic.*

"Let's move," said his uncle, then pointed at the dog. "This is Runt."

"This is what?" asked Jo-Go.

"Sorry," said Todd with a shrug. "I didn't know about the dog."

"Oh?" A look of amusement played across Jo-Go's face.

"Well, Scott and Runt sort of go together. It's a package deal, you see."

Jo-Go scratched his head and winked. "Well, what must be, must be."

Scott understood and breathed a sigh of relief. He made Runt sit for a formal introduction. Runt feebly wagged his tail and held up a paw.

"Of course, this means we've got to make room for an extra passenger," said Todd.

"Of course!" agreed Jo-Go. "That shouldn't be too hard." He waved his arm and headed for the parking lot. "Let's load up and go. Tammie's been running classes for me. And you know how much she enjoys doing that."

Scott studied Jo-Go's face and recognized the sarcasm. *Oh, please do not let Tammie be another "Ark."*

Chapter 10

A New Experience

In the SUV, Scott and Runt sat in the back and Jo-Go and his uncle were up front. The two men started a conversation, and Scott became dizzy trying to understand what they were saying. Finally, he gave up and just enjoyed the countryside.

The California scenery looked nothing like Kansas or Texas. Heavy traffic jammed the freeways and distant mountains marred the horizon. He had never seen a real palm tree before and everything appeared green and colorful.

Soon, they left the freeway and Scott saw a sign identifying a small, dirt road as the entrance to Goen's Glider Academy. The road took them alongside a narrow airstrip. Near the far end of the airstrip, a small airplane sat in front of a hangar.

Scott leaned forward and asked, "You fly?"

"Yeah!" Jo-Go answered enthusiastically.

"You work on the plane a lot?"

"Yeah." Jo-Go glanced at him in the review mirror. "How did you know?"

Scott blushed, not wanting to tell him that he smelled like a mechanic, and just muttered, "A guess."

"It's called a Piper Cub," explained Jo-Go. "It gets the gliders off the ground. Near it is the Buggy."

"A buggy?" Scott raised an eyebrow, wondering if he understood it correctly. He watched the mirror intently for Jo-Go's lips.

Todd turned around, so Scott could see him. "That's the trailer, Scott. It's how we get a glider back to the hangar if it lands somewhere other than here."

Scott caught the words "trailer" and "hangar." Both were nestled at the west end of the airstrip near a ranch house.

Jo-Go pointed at the house. "My place," he explained. "You're welcome any time."

Looking back at the hangar, he could see three gliders inside.

The SUV stopped at a white, frame building. It had a weathered sign over a doorway with the word, OFFICE, printed on it. In front was a small parking lot containing a few cars.

A battered, mobile home rested behind the office building. Through an office window, a long, electric cord extended into it.

While Scott and his uncle carried the baggage into the mobile home, Jo-Go went into one of the training rooms in the office building to take over the ground school instructions.

After dropping his stuff on a spare bed, Scott tugged at his uncle's sleeve and began pointing at the hangar.

"Hey, hold on!" exclaimed Todd. "I'm new at this stuff."

Again, Scott pointed to the hangar outside. "I want to look at the gliders."

"Go for it. I'm going into the office. I'll join you later."

Scott signed 'okay' and headed out the door with Runt close behind.

It was apparent that at one time the hangar had been a barn since it had double sliding doors for the entrance, which were wide open. Scott was absolutely fascinated with the planes.

All three of the gliders were different. The first glider looked tubby. It was a two-seat trainer with wing struts and an extended wing above the pilot's head. The second one was a long, sleek two-seater. The third glider was a one-seater *and* the most interesting. Its trim fuselage was bright red with a wingspan about twenty times as long as it was wide. Seeing as the canopy was open, Scott didn't hesitate to climb inside. Runt hopped right in behind him.

"Hey! I'm not sure you've been approved as a passenger."

Runt whined and licked him on the nose.

"All right, you can stay." Pushing the dog aside, he studied the panel. Most of the indicators he understood—compass, airspeed indicator, altimeter, and something labeled a variometer. He strapped himself in, closed the canopy, and put his feet on the pedals. Runt climbed back into the instructor's seat as Scott grabbed the control stick.

Closing his eyes, Scott imagined flying through the skies, far above the earthbound humans below; free, unchained from gravity, soaring high into the heavens and above the clouds. When the peak of a mighty mountain appeared, he pulled back on the control stick and soared over it, missing the crest by inches. Forests and highways passed below him. Tiny streams and rivers like ribbons wound their way through wooded valleys. Nearby, flocks of birds regarded him; probably wondering what strange sort of creature he was.

He passed through a cloud and became aware of a vibration on the hull as if he had bumped against an eagle in flight...

He opened his eyes and was startled by the appearance of his uncle and a trim, young lady peering through the canopy at him.

Scott smiled sheepishly.

The lady started signing and speaking. "You must be Scott. How are you? I am Tammie."

Todd's mouth dropped open, astonished. "You know sign language?"

"Why, of course." She smiled.

Scott opened the canopy, climbed out of the cockpit, and jumped off the wing in front of Tammie. Using both gesture and voice, he responded with, "Hi!"

"Where's Runt?" asked his uncle.

Scott tooted on his whistle. Runt stuck his head up from the back seat, hopped out, and trotted to his side.

Tammie laughed. "Looks like we have a team all ready to go into action."

Todd just shook his head. "While you three get acquainted, I have my own action to get to." Spinning about, he took off for the office, clapping his hands once.

★ ★ ★

Todd and Jo-Go had heavier class schedules on Mondays and Wednesdays. On those days, Scott spent a lot of time with Tammie. With her, communication was easier. He felt more relaxed and not as hesitant to speak out loud.

"How do you know signing so well?" voiced Scott one time while riding in the car with her.

Tammie turned her head sideways without taking her eyes off the road. "When I was younger," she said, "I had to babysit a deaf cousin."

"But you know sign language better than me."

"I went to a special class. You see, that cousin lived with

us for a long time."

Out the window, Scott could see miles of vineyards. Workers in the fields were harvesting the grapes. He poked Tammie and signed by clasping his hands together. "Uncle Todd married?"

"Just use your voice," she scolded.

"But I'm never sure about it."

"And you never will be if you don't practice. Besides, I have to watch the road." Tammie turned off the farm road onto an expressway and partly faced him, so he could see her mouth.

"Todd is married, but they disagreed. His wife left, and Todd moved here."

"They should talk and com-com-compromise."

"Maybe they tried, but Todd does not want to talk about it."

Scott let that roll around in his head. It was hard to imagine that problems couldn't be worked out when two people really loved one another. Someday, if he could get his strong-headed dad and uncle to sit and talk, he felt they could resolve their differences. After all, they were brothers, and according to Ralston, they "had been friends once."

★ ★ ★

On Wednesday, Tammie went somewhere early. Scott

looked for his uncle but couldn't find him. He picked up a flight instructor's manual and lay on the floor next to his uncle's desk.

Runt sidled up to him and dropped his head on his paws, watching Scott with large, mournful eyes.

"You want attention, huh?" Closing the book, Scott petted Runt and wrestled with him on the floor.

They stopped as Todd walked in. He crouched down to rub Runt's nose. "Scott, I'm sorry that nobody's around to keep you company." Pointing at the book, he asked, "Are you so bored you have to read flight manuals?"

"I'm fine," Scott replied. "I want to learn about gliders."

Runt analyzed Scott's every move; eyes darting back and forth, from Scott to Todd, head tilted as if trying to understand every word.

Todd laughed and clicked his tongue. "Come on, Runt. I'm going up for a little flight practice. Want to come?"

Runt leaped to his feet, his tail pounding against the side of the desk.

"Hey!" Scott scrambled to his feet and pointed to himself.

"Sure, you can come if you want, but I thought you'd rather read about it," he said, yanking his chain.

Scott knew his uncle was teasing and whacked him with the flight manual.

Outside, Jo-Go was busy washing down the Piper Cub. He agreed to take a break and give them a tow.

The glider was a tubby trainer, a Schweizer 2-33 that sat outside the hanger. Todd tugged on the nose handle. Scott grabbed a wing tip and helped guide it out onto the airstrip.

When Todd opened the canopy, Runt climbed into the Instructor's seat.

"A stowaway!" exclaimed Todd. "Are you sure about this?"

Runt's tail indicated he was.

"He will be fine. His old owner was a trucker and took him everywhere with him," Scott explained.

"I bet he'll be more cooperative than some clients you've had," said Jo-Go, on his way to the Piper Cub.

Climbing into the glider, Scott took his place in the student's seat in the front. He had never ridden in a small plane, much less a glider. He was embarking on a new adventure.

Todd squeezed in next to Runt, fastened his seat belt, and closed the canopy, then tapped Scott on the shoulder.

Scott glanced back, reading his words.

"Fasten your seat belt."

"Okay."

"You set?"

Scott gave two thumbs-up.

"All right," said Todd. "Let's go." He waved at Jo-Go to hook on the towline.

The planes rolled down the airstrip. Suddenly, the vibration of the glider's wheels on the runway ceased. Scott beamed from ear to ear as the ground dropped below him.

The glider lifted off the runway, like a kite on the end of a string. It flew about six to ten feet above the ground until the Piper Cub also lifted off. The tow lasted several minutes, attaining a height of about 2500 feet.

Again, Todd tapped Scott on the shoulder and pointed at the release control. "It's time! Jerk on that."

Scott pulled the release and the towline popped off, swinging back to the Piper Cub, which dropped and veered to the left. Todd found an updraft of warm air and pulled the glider into a climb. They leveled off and the ride became very smooth; missing were the vibrations of an engine. It was a special kind of excitement.

They were as high as the clouds. A pair of birds flew below him. *Wow!*

Todd tapped him and waited for him to turn his head. "Better than reading about it, right?"

Scott nodded and signaled with a 'thumbs up.' Once again, he compared his dad and his uncle; so alike and yet so different. Uncle Todd seemed more athletic and full of nervous energy. His dad had always appeared calm and logical. Someday he would get them talking. He just wasn't sure how to go about it.

While looking at the countryside below, he remembered his dad cautioning him about making snap judgments. Maybe he was making one now, but he liked his uncle.

A cold nose planted itself against his neck. Startled, he jerked around to get a lick from an eager, wet tongue. Runt was taking up most of his uncle's lap and trying to wag his tail in a somewhat confined space.

Todd laughed. "I think he would like a better view." He hoisted Runt over the top of the seat into Scott's lap.

I can't believe we are flying! He looked back at his uncle. Remembering Tammie's instructions that he should talk more, he said, "Thanks."

Runt wedged himself into Scott's lap. Being nearly sixty pounds, he was far from little. He looked out the window, apparently interested in the unusual view of things.

"This is fun, isn't it, Runt?"

Runt was panting rapidly, very excited, and again wagged his tail, seemingly in agreement.

Todd guided the glider toward a mountain. Scott felt a sudden twinge of alarm as the giant shadow of a peak engulfed them.

He turned to stare at his uncle. Pointing at the mountain, he exclaimed, "Too high!"

"I'm looking for an updraft that will lift us over."

The mountain loomed large before them and Scott's stomach muscles tightened. Even Runt anxiously looked between Scott and the nearness of the rocks outside the window.

Todd tapped Scott on the shoulder to regain his attention.

"You worry too much."

Abruptly, the glider rose as if aware of the impending danger. It lifted effortlessly and was soon sailing above the summit.

Scott's smile showed his approval, but he clapped as well.

Todd seemed elated at being able to make Scott happy. "It's time to head home." Scott wished they could stay up longer. It was hard to realize they had been up for over an hour.

If you looked up 'happy dog' in the dictionary, Runt's picture would be beside it.

Scott held tight to his best friend as the sailplane glided smoothly downward with his uncle's firm hand at the control. Gently, it landed on the airstrip, like a teenager sneaking back after curfew. Rolling to a stop, Scott unbuckled, opened the canopy, and hopped out with a broad smile on his face, Runt right behind him, an adoring pal. If he could talk, he would probably say, "That was great. What's next?"

Jo-Go met them. "Hey, Scott, I'd ask how you liked it, but your face answers it."

Instead of signing, Scott raised his fist with enthusiasm. "Yes!"

A Dream Comes True

Scott sat in his uncle's empty office and stared through the window at the blue sky. An airplane was making its way across the heavens, leaving a trail of vapors behind it. True, it wasn't a glider, but it made him think about his soaring experience.

Flying in a glider was different than traveling in an airplane. It was more like being a part of the sky; as if he were a bird and the heavens were his playground.

A tap on his shoulder startled him. He jumped to his feet and turned to stare into Tammie's smiling face.

"Sorry to scare you," she said with a laugh, "but I found one."

Scott raised an eyebrow. He moved his hands forward and to the side. "What?"

"A gymnastics club! Remember? You told me how much

fun it was and how you missed it."

Scott felt stunned. *Gymnastics again!* "Yes!" he shouted and wanted to do a back handspring, but there wasn't enough room. "When? Where?"

"Calm down," said Tammie, almost as excited. "It's called The Gymnastics Academy. They meet at two every afternoon until school starts. I stopped by to visit their gym. It's not far. I'll take you."

"Great!" Scott grabbed Tammie and gave her a hug, almost knocking her off her feet.

"Hey!" exclaimed Tammie, kissing him on the forehead. "Now calm down. We have a few things to do." She put her hands on his shoulders and pushed him back at arm's length. "Do you have what you need to do gymnastics?"

Scott rubbed his chin thoughtfully. "I have shorts, T-shirts, and socks." He signed by slicing on one wrist with the other hand. "All I really need are handgrips."

"What's that?"

"They are a kind of glove. I use them to keep from getting blisters on my hands from the high bar."

"Where do we get them?"

"A sports store."

Tammie sat on the edge of the desk. "This club meets in a large warehouse made into a gym. There is a little room inside the front door called The Gym Bag."

"They would have them!"

"All right. We'll plan to go a little early, after lunch."

When Tammie left, Scott ran back into the trailer and changed into a pair of shorts and a T-shirt. Outside, he found a grassy area. With Runt as an enthusiastic critic, he began the stretching exercises. This activity had been an important part of his training.

Runt tried to join in, but Scott made him back off. He whined with concern yet did as he was told. He lay a few yards away, watching with large sad eyes.

Runt had to stay behind when Scott and Tammie went to the Gymnastics Academy. Arriving a few minutes early, they dropped into The Gym Bag for handgrips and a small duffel bag. They located the boys' coach who was watching his team do their stretching exercises.

Tammie introduced Scott. "Scott's been a member of a gymnastics team in Texas. He's now staying with us and would like to try out."

The coach held out his hand to Scott. "I'm Sam."

"Hi." Scott shook hands, then noticed a couple of girls performing in a separate area of the gym.

A second later, Tammie tapped his shoulder and gestured at the coach. "He was asking you something." She turned to the coach and explained. "Scott is deaf, but he often understands by reading your lips."

Coach Sam made eye contact with Scott and slowly repeated his questions. "How–old–are–you? How–long–were–

you-in-gym-nas-tics?"

"I'm thirteen," responded Scott, signing as he spoke from force of habit. "I've been in gymnastics for six years; four years on a team."

Sam, speaking directly but less forcefully, asked, "We're getting ready for competition. If your skills are up to par, you're welcome to join us."

"I can do it," said Scott, signing with both fists.

The coach raised his thumb. "All right! I like that attitude." He pointed. "As you can see, the guys are warming up. Go for it!"

"Thanks!"

Tammie grabbed him by the shoulder. "I'll be back after your workout." She waved as she walked out the door.

Scott waved back and grabbed his gym bag, then trotted to the back area to join a group about his age. They were going through various stages of their stretching exercises.

One redheaded guy with freckles walked over to him and stuck out his hand. "Hi, I'm Sandy." He pointed to a larger, black boy nearby. "That's Josh."

Josh raised a hand in greeting while stretching out. "Howdy."

Sandy laughed. "As you can tell, he's from Texas."

"Not everybody who uses southern slang is from Texas," said Josh, "but in this case, he's right."

"Hey, I'm from Texas, too."

A stern-looking boy with black, piercing eyes made a comment that Scott couldn't read.

Sandy poked him. "That's Paul. He said he never met a Texan who knew much about gymnastics."

Scott turned to face Paul. "Well, you're meeting one now."

"We'll see about that." Sandy stepped in front of Scott and mouthed, "Don't pay him any attention. He thinks he's better than everybody else."

Scott took note but continued his stretching.

Shortly, Coach Sam joined the group and gathered them around him. "Fellows, this is Scott. He's going to work out with us. He's been on a team in Texas and has a special challenge because he's deaf."

Sandy piped up. "Coach, that can be an advantage when you start yelling at him."

Most everyone laughed.

Scott saw the comment. The guys were a lot like the team in Texas.

"Seriously," Sam went on, "always get Scott's attention and talk directly at him when you have something to say. Just being a gymnast is hard enough without having to work around other problems as well."

Just about all the guys agreed.

"Okay, let's go to work!"

During the workout, Scott discovered that most of guys accepted him without question. This became especially true

after he had proven his skills were about par with theirs.

He was elated when Tammie came to pick him up after practice with Runt. Forgetting all about signing, he told her all about the workout. Runt whined and nuzzled Scott's hand. He'd missed his pal.

★★★

After overcoming the soreness that came during the first few days, he improved greatly, and his skills were honed with Sam's help.

One day, while passing through his uncle's office, he found Runt lying next to the desk; a pitiful sight with big mournful eyes as if to say, "I miss you."

"Runt, listen." Scott dropped to his knees and took the dog's head between his hands. "I know I don't see as much of you as I used to, but this is something I have to do. It's something I'm good at." Then it occurred to him that that was just like his dad. *Uncanny!*

Runt turned his head as if absorbing everything Scott said, then reached up and licked him on the chin.

"I knew you'd understand." Scott hugged him. "We can still play together. I promise."

★ ★ ★

One Monday, after a hard practice, Coach Sam pulled Scott aside and squatted in front of him. "Been working out with us over a week now."

Scott nodded expectantly.

"When's the last time you competed?"

"A long time."

"Got a meet coming up this Saturday. If you compete as a member of our team, you could help us score well enough to be eligible for the California State Competition. Would you like to try?"

Scott almost burst with excitement.

Sam handed him a pair of shorts and a shirt. "Here's a team outfit. See if you can fit into it."

When Tammie picked him up that evening, Scott was so excited that he shouted her name. His face flushed at her look of alarm. After throwing his gym bag into the back of the pickup, he began rapidly speaking and signing about the upcoming competition and wanted her and his uncle to be there when he did.

She raised her palm for him to slow down. "Slow down! I can't follow you."

Scott took a deep cleansing breath, then retold what he had said.

"That's fabulous!" she exclaimed. "I'll be there!"

When Todd heard of the event, he said, "There's no way I would miss this. I'll see if I can't rearrange my Saturday classes. Maybe I can talk Jo-Go and Runt into looking after things while we're gone."

Runt looked as if he had lost his best friend. A pang of guilt hit Scott like someone had just slapped him in the face. He squatted in front of his best friend and ruffled his ears. "Look, I know I promised to spend more time with you, but this is the chance of a lifetime."

Runt whined.

"Gotta go!" Scott kissed him on the head and headed for a shower before supper.

The Competition

As the big day arrived, everyone gathered in the gymnasium. All six apparatuses for the guys to compete on had been set up on the floor. The auditorium was a whir of excitement. Scott and the other members of the team stretched out at one end of the gym. Soon, they lined up with the others in front of the bleachers.

An announcer introduced each team, everyone stood for the National Anthem, then the events got underway.

Scott's first event was the vault. He moved to the starting position. Coach Sam adjusted the springboard in front of the vaulting horse and gave him a thumbs-up.

Scott responded in kind, then faced the judges and waited for them to look up so he could signal he was ready.

He quickly gauged the vibes from the other members of

the team. Sandy and Josh waved and gave him a thumbs-up, just like his teammates in Texas had done.

Tammie and his uncle stood in the bleachers cheering. The only one missing was his dad.

He beamed, confident but tense; adrenaline rushing forth. The judges looked up, and Scott raised his hand. The head judge gave the go-ahead and Scott stepped onto the runway.

Blinking his eyes, he took a deep breath and riveted his concentration on the springboard in front of the horse. The movements of the others faded as he poised on his toes and began the long sprint down the runway. Carefully calculating the length of each stride, he hit the springboard squarely and cartwheeled across the top of the horse. After twisting a quarter turn into a backward somersault, he landed on his feet and his arms shot up in completion.

Scott returned to his team and found himself facing a host of congratulations. Sandy poked him and pointed at the scoreboard.

9.6.

Raising his fist, Scott shouted, "Yes!"

His uncle and Tammie were standing and applauding with great enthusiasm. He half-smiled and his face flushed. If his dad could have been there, it would have been perfect.

At the awards ceremony, the presenter was facing the audience with his back to the competitors, but his best friends, Josh and Sandy, nudged him when his name was called.

Scott received a first-place ribbon for his efforts on the vault. Several members of the team were recognized for events on the high bar, floor, pommel horse, the rings, and parallel bars. The team scored well enough in all events to place third in the all-around category. This made them eligible to compete in the state competition.

After the awards were presented and the meet was over, the coach gathered the team about him. He complimented and encouraged them to perfect their skills for the state competition.

When Scott left the gym, he strolled into the parking lot behind the school, searching for Tammie and his uncle, his head full of dreams. Someday, he would qualify all the way to a national meet. He could just see himself at the awards ceremony...

His name would flash on a screen. He would walk across the floor and climb to the highest level on the stand. There, an official would hold up a bright, silver medal suspended on a red, white, and blue ribbon. He would bend down and the ribbon would be placed over his head. He would look around and see his dad, his uncle, Tammie, and Jo-Go. They would be applauding and—

Someone grabbed his shoulders and jerked him back as a car passed just inches in front of him. He caught his breath and his heart beat wildly as he turned to meet the stern gaze of his uncle.

"Dreaming is all right, but not while walking through a parking lot." His uncle hugged him, then pushed him back and firmly grabbed Scott's head, forcing him to watch what he said. "It's a good thing I came to check on you. Be careful. We love you and don't want anything to happen to you." With that, he relaxed a little. "Besides, I wouldn't know what to tell your dad."

Scott understood completely. His dad would have said some of the same things. Using his voice, Scott said, "I'll be more careful." Then he became quite animated, saying,

"I did it! I did as well as anyone, even if I couldn't hear them."

Todd searched his eyes. "Is that what all of this is about? Don't you realize folks would like you even if you didn't do as well?"

"Sure," Scott shrugged, "but you're my uncle and—"

"What difference do you think that makes?" Todd pointed back at the gym. "If you scored last place, do you think your team would tease you and no longer be your friends? Think about it."

Scott did but remembered how kind several of the guys had been, even when he screwed up in practice.

Todd clamped a hand on Scott's shoulder, then bent over to look at him eye to eye. "They like you for *who* you are, not for how successful you are."

Scott thought about Rustie; how she'd shown her

concern, even when recovering her bike that he had taken. *That's what a true friend is like.*

"In fact," continued his uncle, "I know of a special four-footed friend of yours that could care less about your gymnastics. He likes you in spite of the way you ignore him."

Scott gasped. "Runt! I hadn't intended to—"

His uncle raised an eyebrow.

"I'll make it up to him. I promise! And he isn't the only one." Scott put his fingers to his lips and slapped his fist, then grabbed his uncle by the hand. "Thanks."

"For what? Pulling you out from in front of a car?"

"That, and everything else."

Pointing at the SUV where Tammie was waiting, he said, "I think there's someone else you ought to say something to as well."

"Yeah, you're right." Scott took off running.

Tammie studied their faces as they approached. "Is everything all right?"

"Just fine!" He hugged her and signed 'thanks.' "Thanks! Thanks for everything."

"Sure, but what brought this on?"

"Nothing. It was just something I needed to do."

"Everything is great," said Todd, winking at Scott.

Runt barked his greeting as they drove up in front of the ranch house. While Todd and Tammie parked, the dog pounced on Scott; attacked him with his tongue as if the boy had just returned from a long absence. They wrestled on the front lawn until exhausted.

"Well, Runt, I did all right at the meet." Scott rubbed the dog's furry coat. "I proved I could do as well as anyone. And I promise—for real this time—I'll not ignore you like that again." He hugged Runt's neck. "Maybe with a little practice we could make a gymnast out of you, too."

Scott caught sight of his uncle waving at him from the front porch. Scrambling to his feet, Scott trotted over to him.

Uncle Todd looked serious. "Scott, you got a letter from your dad."

The Unexpected

Scott studied the envelope. His dad's neatly penned handwriting stuck out like a neon sign.

Todd clapped him on the shoulder. "Aren't you going to open it?"

"I'm afraid he's angry."

"With you?" He regarded him with a raised eyebrow. "Why? It was your grandmother's idea to send you here."

"But it was my fault."

"Your fault? Maybe, but your grandmother overreacted from what Ralston told me. Still, you'll never know what your dad thinks unless you open the envelope. I'll be in the office if you need to talk."

After he left, Scott slowly tore off one end of the envelope and pulled out the letter.

Dear Scott,

I finally know where you are. Every time I called your grandmother, she said you were out somewhere, so I talked with Ralston. He told me everything.

I miss you and regret how things worked out. I can't get back to the States just yet, but I will soon. Sorry I never told you about your Uncle Todd. He and I have our differences, but I know he'll do his best by you.

I have a surprise, but it can wait until I see you in person, which ought to be within a couple of weeks.

Take care of yourself. See you soon.

    Dad

"Yes!" Scott thrust his fist in the air. Finally, his dad will come, and he didn't seem upset. Maybe he and Uncle Todd will sit down and talk. Also, it was already the first of August. That meant school was just around the corner, and his future was uncertain.

He got an envelope and paper from Tammie. Replying to his dad's letter, he explained what had happened to cause his grandmother to send him to California. He also told him about the gymnastics club and his experience flying in a glider.

★ ★ ★

The next morning, Scott grabbed a can of polish and followed his uncle to the hangar. He helped him move the Adventurer out in front of the door. "Uncle Todd, this glider is great."

"Yes, it *is* special."

"Why?"

"I designed it." Todd brushed his hand over the bright red wing. "When I was a boy, my dad arranged a glider ride for us. Since then, I have wanted to build my own."

"Dad never told me."

"That's not surprising." Todd chuckled. "Your dad and I have always had different interests."

"You mean he didn't like flying in a glider?"

"Oh, he enjoyed it, but he soon forgot about it and went on to other things."

Scott dreamily ran his hand over the surface of the wing. "It's pretty."

"It's more than that. It's the fastest glider in the country."

"You're going to race it?"

"You bet!"

Jo-Go entered the hangar gloomily and handed Todd an envelope. "This came for you; forwarded from your old apartment. It looks kind of important."

Todd read the return address. "From a lawyer?"

As his uncle tore open the envelope, Scott raised his hand to Jo-Go in greeting. He rubbed a bit of polish on the shiny,

119

red fuselage while watching their faces.

Todd reread the thin, official-looking paper, then said, "Well, she finally did it. Gloria's filing for divorce."

"Sorry to hear that. Anything I can do?"

"Not really. I knew it was coming."

He addressed Scott, "Let's quit for now. I feel like going up for a short flight. How about it?"

"Sure!" Scott pointed at his pal. "Can Runt come, too?"

Todd shrugged. "Why not?"

"Todd…" began Jo-Go.

Todd turned to his partner. "I don't have any more classes for the day. How about a tow?"

Jo-Go gave him a questioning look. "You sure?"

"Yeah, I think Scott and I deserve a little relaxation away from everybody, at least for a short while."

"All right." Jo-Go headed for the Piper Cub.

Scott scrutinized his uncle's downcast eyes, his knitted brow. He also seemed tired.

Todd waved his arm. "C'mon! Help me with the 2-32."

Hustling to the side of the tubby-looking glider, Scott pushed. His uncle grabbed the nose handle and pulled toward the runway.

Jo-Go snapped on the towline and hopped into the Piper Cub. Scott, Todd, and Runt scrambled aboard and buckled in, closing the canopy. With a thumbs-up, they raced down the runway, the glider lifted, then Jo-Go raised the nose of his plane and left the ground. After both aircraft had leveled off, Scott waited for Todd to signal him to release the towline.

Waving at Jo-Go, he jerked on the release. The towline popped off, flying behind the Piper Cub. Jo-Go waved acknowledgment and made a diving turn back for the airfield.

After Todd gave a thumbs-up, he adjusted his harness and sat back to study the clouds and the ground below. In a moment, he felt a tap on his shoulder.

Turning in his seat, he came face to face with Runt, ears erect, crowded into his uncle's lap and taking up space.

"Don't have a whole lot of room," said Todd. "Can you take him?"

"Sure."

Todd passed him over the back of the seat. Runt playfully grabbed Scott's hand in his mouth.

With a laugh, Scott stroked the dog and turned to gaze at his uncle's face. "You okay?"

"Yeah, even with all the company."

Scott could tell he wasn't angry despite his words.

Todd continued, "At least, Runt has a code of loyalty a lot stronger than some people. Take Gloria, I knew we got married too fast, but she could've given me more than a few months."

That was a lot to follow, but Scott understood that his uncle was upset about his wife leaving him. He fondled Runt's ears who was fixated with a hawk flying nearby.

Finding a thermal, his uncle spiraled into a climb before heading north above the mountains that overlooked the ocean. Little white clouds floated aimlessly about. With the cities in the valleys below, the mountains before them, and the ocean on the horizon, it was peaceful and exciting.

Scott studied the passing scenery beneath them. In a few minutes, he turned and said, "We've gone pretty far."

Todd checked his watch. "You're right. It's time to head back." Leveling off at 4000 feet, he veered the glider back to the windward side of the coastal hills to take advantage of the slope winds. He tapped his nephew on the shoulder and pointed. "Just look at that ocean and beach, isn't it grand? It was on a beach like that where I asked Gloria to marry me and..." He choked a little and his eyes moistened.

Scott was trying to watch what was said but missed some of the words when his uncle turned from him.

"Now, the question is, what do I do next?" asked Todd, not necessarily to Scott; no, more to himself.

Hugging Runt, it made him sad to think about his uncle's problem, especially when there was no way he could help.

Runt peered back at Todd and cocked his head to one side like he always did when it seemed that someone was talking to him.

Suddenly, his uncle grabbed Scott's shoulder. Todd's face had turned an ashen white and he clutched at his chest. "My jacket!" he gasped. "Where's my jacket?"

Alarmed, Scott didn't understand. He pointed to the back and searched under his seat.

Todd gasped, "Oh, my God! The truck! They're in the truck!"

Panicking, Scott asked, "What's in the truck?"

"My pills!" exclaimed Todd. "In my jacket!" With that he grunted and bent over double. "The controls! Take them."

Scott felt a streak of panic. What could *he* do? He had sat in a few classes, learning about gliders, even landed one during a training session, but it had been for fun with his uncle guiding him, step by step.

This was different.

Shoving Runt to one side, he grabbed the control stick with both hands.

Don't panic, he told himself. *You can remember what to do. Just be calm.*

Frightened, he yelled, "Uncle Todd, what do I do?"

Todd was still clutching his chest, his face a sickly white.

Knowing there would be no help coming from there, Scott took in a big gulp of air. "We need help! There's no time to get home." He looked back at his uncle. "Uncle Todd!" he yelled, "Stay with me!" *What do I do? Oh, God, please help us!*

His uncle was slumped over, lips moving, but if he said anything, it was so mumbled that there was no way it could be read.

Runt whined and wagged his tail, then pressed his nose against the window as if trying to help find a landing place.

Images of crashing through the tree tops flashed through Scott's head. He anxiously scanned the area below and saw a level area between a pair of hills.

Glancing at Runt, he exclaimed, "Look! There's a pasture over there. Might be rough, but better than the treetops."

He took a deep breath. Adjusting his seat strap, he clutched the control stick so tightly with both hands that his arms shook.

I've got to remember. Relax! he reminded himself. *Uncle Todd talked me through it once. I've just got to remember what he told me.*

He studied the area. "All right, Runt. Stay against the window and don't get in the way. I'm going to make a circle and loop in from the north. The speed's got to stay at fifty."

Runt panted heavily.

"Don't worry. I know what I'm doing… I think. We'll make it." As if to convince himself, he said it again. "I can do this!"

He guided the sailplane into a wide loop, allowing it to gently descend. Approaching the pasture, he lowered the ailerons, dropping the speed as much as he dared. Below him, the ground rushed past as if he were riding the angry waters of a river. It was as if he were about to plunge over the edge of a waterfall.

Praying, *Dear God, please be my guide,* he gently shoved the stick forward.

Chapter 14

The Landing

The glider hit the ground with a jolt and bounced across the rough terrain. Near the end of the pasture, it struck a boulder, flipping the tail up in the air. The glider fell upside down against a tree. A cloud of dust rose to mark its resting place.

Scott blinked his eyes to get his bearings. Everything was upside-down, with Runt whining and wedged on his chest, but he was alive.

The glider! I landed it!

He wrestled with the shoulder harness. Undoing it, he flipped into an upright position on the canopy. The glider's tail rested against the tree, suspending the canopy off the ground far enough for him to open it.

Coughing from the dust, Scott dropped to the ground with a grunt; Runt right behind him with a yelp. He looked back through the canopy where his uncle dangled from his harness. Struggling back into the cockpit, he reached up to shake his uncle's shoulder.

"Uncle Todd! Uncle Todd!"

He placed a shaking hand on his uncle's neck and thought he felt a pulse. Puffing as if he had just finished a marathon, he dropped back to the ground, thinking of what to do next.

Two boys raced across the meadow; one older than Scott, the other younger.

"We saw you crash," said the older boy. "Are you okay?"

Scott pointed to his chest and nodded 'yes,' then pointed at Todd saying, "Something's wrong with my uncle."

While the younger boy stood in shock, the older one scrambled inside to look Todd over. He dropped back out of the glider and said to the younger boy, "He's breathing. Joe, go call 911."

Joe darted away at a dead run.

Scott and the older boy loosened Todd from his harness. They gently pulled him out of the canopy and lowered him to the ground.

In a short while, an ambulance rumbled along the dirt road on the other side of the fence, its lights flashing. A battered old pickup and a police car rumbled along behind it.

Joe and a stout, balding man hopped out. The man pulled out a key ring and unlocked the gate, allowing the ambulance and police car to enter. The vehicles thundered across the pasture toward the glider.

Scott thanked the boys as the EMTs lifted Todd onto a stretcher, then loaded him into the ambulance, working on him the whole time.

The police officer put his arm around Scott, saying, "Come on, I will take you to the hospital. Don't you worry none. Your uncle will be all right."

Pulling into the ER right behind the ambulance, the officer escorted Scott to the waiting area.

Approaching the counter, Scott showed Tammie's name and phone number to the lady. He was so glad she had insisted he carry the information in his wallet for emergencies. He pleaded, "Please call."

The nurse raised an eyebrow to the officer and pointed to the opposite wall, saying, "The phone's over there."

Scott shook his head and pointed to his ears, speaking and signing, "I can't."

The officer said, "I think he is deaf."

Understanding, she picked up the desk phone, moving constantly, doing one thing or another as she spoke, making it impossible to read what she was saying. After she hung up, she looked directly at him and announced, "Mrs. Goens is on the way."

Scott signed and said, "Thank you." Then the officer led him to a chair to wait, staying with him until Tammie arrived.

This can't be happening. Every time I get close to someone, something bad happens. First, my mom, then the gym team, then Dad left for the other side of the planet, then because of The Ark, Rustie and Ralston… and now this! I am a jinx. Maybe I should be a hermit, go off somewhere, and learn how to live alone.

In what seemed like forever to Scott, Tammie rushed through the automatic doors of the ER, straight to the front desk. Seeing Scott, she grabbed him in an embrace, then tilted his chin up. "Have faith. Your uncle is in the best of hands.

"Thanks for staying with him, Officer."

The policeman simply tipped his hat and left, saying they would be in touch.

Suddenly, Scott wanted to hold Runt. Tears filled his eyes as he signed emphatically, "Runt! I forgot about Runt! He's still out there!"

For a moment, Tammie stood speechless at this new piece of information. Gaining control, she said, "Don't you worry none. We'll find him."

Scott hugged Tammie as if he were afraid she might abandon him like everyone else. His world was falling apart. *How could this be happening? I wish Dad was here!*

Moments later, he wiped his eyes and looked up into Tammie's face. "Uncle Todd, is he okay?"

"He's in intensive care, but out of danger for now. He's doing fine."

Scott searched for the truth in Tammie's face. "What was

wrong? He was looking for pills."

Before she could answer, Jo-Go walked up to them in the lobby. "Tammie, I've talked with the doctor and the police, and I've given them all the information I could. The police have cleared us to move the glider. They gave me a copy of their report. It tells where it went down. Maybe Scott will go with me to get the Buggy and help load it? What do you say?"

"Runt's there," Tammie said.

"We'll get him, too. Come on, Scott, there's nothing more we can do here."

Scott looked to Tammie for approval.

She signed, "Don't worry."

As they walked toward the truck, Scott could see how concerned Jo-Go was; eyebrows scrunched, a distant stare. They drove to the ranch house in silence. After attaching the Buggy, they headed north.

Jo-Go drove as if in a trance.

Scott kept his thoughts to himself as they drove past the orchards. *Uncle Todd must be in bad shape if he's in intensive care. What would happen if he didn't make it out of the hospital? That could mean Kansas again... for a lifetime. Also, Runt will be frightened all by himself.* He shook his head. *That's not going to happen. I'll find Runt. Dad spent his life traveling. Maybe moving from place to place is the answer. Like a hobo, I could go it alone. It would be an adventure. I could hop box cars and travel wherever the train goes, just like on TV.*

A tap on the shoulder interrupted his wandering mind. "Are we near?" Jo-Go asked, as he consulted a map lying on the seat between them.

Scott scanned the countryside, then recognized the field where the glider had crashed and pointed to a dirt road that led by it.

When they arrived at a gate, Scott motioned Jo-Go to stop. "I must know. What is wrong with Uncle Todd?"

"Todd's not hurt from the landing," said Jo-Go. "It's his heart the doctors are worried about."

"Why?"

"He's been taking medicine, and we didn't know it." Jo-Go pounded the steering wheel. "Why wouldn't he tell us? His best friends?" In shock, nothing outside the windshield registered. "What if this had happened while he was taking a client up for the first time?" Then he asked Scott. "What if you had never landed a glider? Are you okay?"

Scott read enough words to understand. "Maybe, he didn't want us to worry." He hopped out of the truck and unlatched the gate, then got back in, thinking repeatedly as they drove across the pasture, *Uncle Todd will get better and we will find Runt.*

At the crash site, they looked for any sign of Runt. Scott called out the dog's name, again and again to no avail.

They checked the damage to the glider. Scott helped take off the wings and tie them, the canopy, and the fuselage onto the Buggy.

Finally, after one last search for Runt, they left.

After pulling through the gate, Jo-Go got out to latch it. Positioning himself behind the wheel, he made no movement to put it in gear. Placing a hand on Scott's shoulder, he said slowly and distinctly, "Look, buddy, I know you're worried about your uncle and Runt. Please understand. No matter what happens, you can stay with us as long as you want."

Tears trickled down Scott's cheeks, knowing Jo-Go meant well, but he didn't want to think about those things right now.

Jo-Go put the SUV in 'drive' and headed for the freeway. Scott felt a nudge. "Don't worry about Runt. We'll find him."

"We would have if he was hurt," Scott answered. "Maybe he's going home, you know, back to the airfield."

"It's a long way."

"He could do it." Scott said it out loud, more to convince himself than Jo-Go. He knew stories about animals finding their way over much greater distances. However, these dogs had retraced the route that got them lost. He didn't know of any that returned home after being dropped into a strange place from the sky. *How could I have forgotten about my best friend?*

At the hangar, Scott and Jo-Go unhitched the Buggy and pulled off the parts of the 2-32. It took the rest of the afternoon to put the glider back together. They repaired it and rolled it into the hangar.

With Scott by his side, Jo-Go called Tammie at the hospital. She told him that Todd was stabilized, resting, and would not be allowed visitors, so she was coming home. She planned to contact their clients and postpone the Thursday morning classes, then return the next day.

Scott sighed with relief. Again, he thought about what he would do if he had to go back to Kansas. Tearing out a page from his uncle's notebook, he began a list. If things didn't work out, he could gather what he needed and head for the rails.

With no further word, Scott showered and went to bed, an uncertain future flitting through his mind.

★ ★ ★

As soon as the sun breached the horizon, he and Tammie headed to the hospital.

Arriving, they were told good news! Todd had been moved out of intensive care and could have visitors for short periods of time.

Entering his uncle's room, Scott's spirits soared! He sat on the edge of the bed where he could watch what was being said.

Todd's eyes seemed bluer, contrasting sharply with the ghostly pallor of his face. He whispered, "Scott, are you all right?"

"I'm fine."

"I'm very proud of you landing the glider."

"No, I crashed it."

"You did great!"

Todd addressed Tammie, "I'm ready to go home."

"Why didn't you tell us about your heart?" asked Tammie, ignoring him, visibly perturbed.

"Would you and Jo-Go have agreed to let me work with you if I had?"

Tammie opened her mouth, looking like a codfish, but said nothing.

"You've answered my question."

"You can always do more sales and the ground school instructions," said Tammie. "Leave the flying to us."

"Yeah, I guess so." Todd's expression made him look like a bird whose wings had been clipped.

"Aw, come on, you know good and well what happened up there could have been a disaster."

"I've always had my medicine, except this one time." Todd's head swiveled from Scott to Tammie. "You're right, of course. I understand. I'll stick to the ground school from now on." He fidgeted a little. "But there's one thing I must do. I've had a dream of building the fastest glider in the country since I was a kid. The Adventurer will be ready for the annual state competition, and I'm going to fly her." Tammie started to say something, knowing the FAA (Federal Aviation Administration) would be notified, but Todd interrupted, "Don't worry. I'll make sure my medicine is with me." He

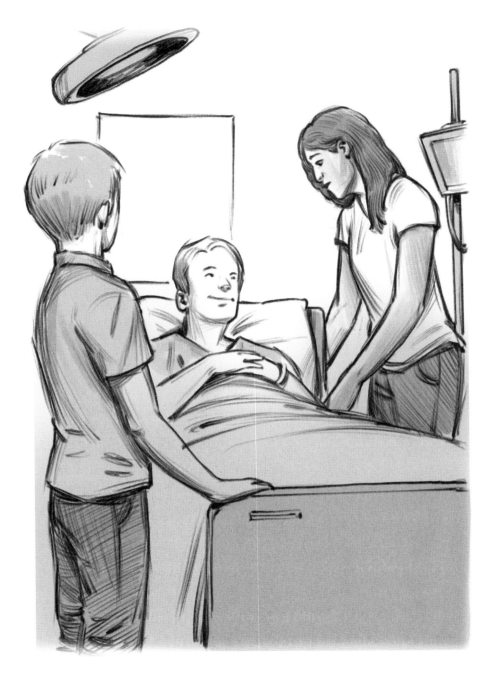

asked Scott. "How's Runt?"

"Todd, the dog wasn't there," Tammie answered for him.

"But we will find him," Scott assured him.

Todd did not like the sound of that. "He might be hurt or dazed. Have you picked up the glider?"

Tammie touched his arm. "Jo-Go and Scott got it yesterday. They didn't find Runt. He could be on the way home. We just don't know."

"Maybe he was frightened and is hiding," said Todd. "Still, we can check with the farms around there. Put up signs around town."

The nurse stuck her head in the door to let them know that visiting time was over.

"Take care," said Scott, giving him a hug.

"Don't worry. I will. Find Runt."

"Look, don't worry about it. We will." Tammie leaned over and gave him a kiss on the cheek.

Scott gave his uncle an encouraging smile as they went out the door. He knew it wouldn't help for him to know how broken-hearted he was.

After leaving the hospital, Scott directed Tammie to the place where the glider had crashed. Again, they searched the pasture and the surrounding area.

They were about to give up when Scott remembered the whistle that Rustie's mother had given him. He pulled it out from under his shirt and blew it as hard as he could. He continued blowing as he and Tammie moved from one area to another in a broad path around the crash site.

A dark shadow streaked out from among the brush.

Scott caught his breath, stumbled backwards, and threw up his hands for protection. Too slow, his concerns were instantly forgotten as Runt pounced on his chest and licked his face.

Scott hugged his best pal and wrestled with him. "I'm so glad to see you."

Runt licked Scott's face as he giggled and hooted and hugged his best friend.

"Wish all our problems could have a happy ending," said Tammie, patting Runt on the head. "Come on, you two. Let's head for home."

Chapter 15

A Revelation

Five days later, Jo-Go, Tammie, and Scott went to the hospital. Todd appeared to be in a good mood. He had been informed about Runt's return and the fact he was being released.

"Hi, guys!" He greeted them with a big smile and exclaimed, "Now, get me out of here!"

"But there's paperwork—" began Jo-Go.

"That's taken care of!" shouted Todd. "This is a hospital. I don't belong here. Let's go!"

A nurse rolled a wheelchair into his room and put a stop to the hurry. "Hold on! The only way you get out of here is on wheels. Now hop in."

"Zush!" Todd threw his hands up in the air. "Rules! I hate 'em."

Tammie and Jo-Go glanced at each other, both silently saying, *He's back!*

In spite of his gruff manner, Todd did as instructed and was promptly wheeled out to the SUV, with Scott walking right beside him.

"Take care of yourself and do what you have been told," said the nurse, then rolled the empty chair back into the hospital.

Todd muttered, climbing into the passenger side of the SUV, "I wonder if *all* their nurses get drill sergeant training."

Tammie walked around to the driver's side and Jo-Go and Scott got in back. En route, Todd said very little, except to talk about some business regarding sales and Runt.

At the ranch house, Tammie moved Todd into the guest room, and fussed over him like he was a long-lost relative. That evening, after a reunion with Runt, Todd sat for the evening meal with Jo-Go, Tammy, and Scott.

Jo-Go, very curious and quite concerned, asked, "I still don't understand. How long have you had this heart condition?"

"About a year. I didn't want to lose my pilot's license."

"I find it hard to believe you kept it from us all this time."

Todd set his fork down to explain. "The doctor said it was something I'd probably have to control with medication for the rest of my life. Now, if I hadn't forgotten my medicine—"

"We still wouldn't know," scolded Tammie, pushing

her chair back from the table to get up, "and we're your best friends. If you suddenly had a massive heart attack, we wouldn't have known what was going on." At the doorway to the kitchen, she added, "And like I said, if you were flying with an untrained client when this happened, it could have been a disaster. That's not only dangerous for everyone involved, but also a liability to us."

Todd refused to lift his eyes from the table like a schoolboy being reprimanded by a teacher. "I know," he said meekly. "I hadn't thought—"

"That's for sure!" Tammie exclaimed, striding out of the room.

Scott wanted his uncle to know how he felt and rapped on the table to get his attention. "Take care of yourself," he said.

"Don't worry. I will."

Jo-Go got up and placed a hand on Todd's shoulder. "Anything you need?"

"Naw, I'm fine."

"There wasn't much damage to the trainer," Jo-Go reassured him. "She'll be as good as new with just a little touch-up here and there."

Scott understood the conversation and grabbed his uncle's arm. "I'll help! We'll do it together."

"Okay," replied Todd. "With all of you, how could I go wrong?"

"I don't remember locking up the hangar," said Jo-Go,

pushing on the screen door. "Be back in a minute."

Todd moved to the porch to sit on the swing while Scott plopped down on the steps to gaze at the shadows; Runt, his constant companion, by his side.

A few thunderheads were building in the east. The shades of color on them slowly darkened as the sun moved toward the horizon.

His uncle reached over and tapped him on the shoulder. "What are you thinking?"

"I wonder how Dad is doing," Scott replied.

"Your dad's quite resourceful," said his uncle. "He can take care of himself in most any situation."

"I miss him."

"I understand. Runt is also very important, isn't he?"

Scott nodded.

"Otherwise, you wouldn't have brought him to California. If your grandmother had not called after the fireworks incident, I wouldn't have had the chance to get to know either you or Runt."

Scott read his lips, mouth agape.

"Yes," continued Todd, "Ralston told me what your grandmother didn't. Isn't it funny how an animal can influence the lives of so many people?"

Scott was so glad his uncle approved of him being there.

The sun had sunk below the horizon when Jo-Go returned. He nudged Scott to get his attention. "Good night, everyone," he said.

"Wish you the same," replied Todd, as Scott echoed the statement with a gesture. "I'm feeling a little tired, too. It's been an event-filled day." He got up from the swing, signed 'good night' to Scott, and gave him a brief hug, then followed Jo-Go into the ranch house.

As Scott watched them enter the house, he reflected on how his uncle's movements and the way he walked were just like his dad's. Even the brief hug and the way he'd signed 'good night' were exactly how his dad would have.

Elbows on knees, fist under his chin, he studied the stars. *Maybe they had shone in Japan before, and Dad had seen the same ones.* Scott hadn't heard from him for over a week and his imagination soared. *Could he have been captured by a band of renegades? Maybe he was being held somewhere for ransom.*

Focusing on the North Star, Scott whispered, "Watch over my dad. Guide him safely wherever he goes."

The star seemed to twinkle as if responding to his plea.

Scott smiled at the thought, then he and Runt retired for the night.

★ ★ ★

"I'm fine!" Todd defended himself. "I have my medicine and have been taking it as instructed. I can't stop living just because I had a heart attack."

"I agree," argued Jo-Go, "but you could slow down a bit."

Scott was concerned with this exchange. Not only was he worried about his uncle, but his own future was one big question mark. The California State Gymnastics Competition would be held in another week, and he had heard nothing from his dad except for that one letter.

When he mentioned this later that night, Tammie and his uncle begged him to be patient.

"Look, Scott," said Todd, "you know you're welcome here."

"Will you ask my dad to let me stay here when he has to go again?" Scott asked.

Todd dropped his eyes. "I'm not sure I'm the right person for that. But if you want, I'll try."

After supper, Scott dug out a piece of paper with Rustie's email address. He wrote a long email, telling her about the gliders and how he won a ribbon in a gymnastics meet.

A few hours later, he received a reply informing him that the McAtees were selling the service station. They were moving to some little town in New Jersey to care for a sick relative.

If he were forced to return to his grandmother's, Chelsey, Kansas would be a very lonely place indeed.

Chapter 16

A Guest

The countdown was on until the state gymnastics competition. Scott and Runt followed Todd into the hangar as they often did. Being late afternoon, the western sky was glowing with color. Todd climbed inside the glider to check the electronics.

Runt trotted over to a rug and curled up in front of a small electric heater they used to cut through a chill that settled in from the nearby mountains. It was his favorite place to lie and watch whoever was in the hangar, even when it wasn't on.

Scott jumped in alarm as his uncle jerked his head up, bumping it on a control panel.

Tammie stepped inside the door. "Whoops! Sorry about that!"

"When you yell like that, you scare the life out of me," said Todd, rubbing his head. "What's happening?"

Scott signed 'hello' to Tammie and moved around to where he could watch what was being said.

"Todd, you remember how you were worried about Scott not hearing from his dad?"

"So?"

"You can stop worrying. He just called! He's on the way from the airport."

"Who? Charles?" Todd's mouth dropped open. "On the way? Here?"

Tammie thought his reaction was the funniest thing all day. "That's the only brother you have, isn't it, silly?"

Scott bounced up and down. "Dad? Coming here?"

"He should be here in an hour or so."

"That *is* a surprise." Todd turned a little pale. "What did he say?"

"He was concerned about Scott. I told him his son was fine. He rented a car at the airport. Since you moved back to the trailer, I offered our spare room for the night."

"Oh, wow!" Todd reached for the pocket that contained his pills, then apparently change his mind, and instead took a big breath of air.

Scott noticed this as a cloud covered the sun. *Maybe Uncle Todd is not as well as we all thought.* He leaned against the sailplane and interpreted their conversation.

"Now, look," Tammie said, "I know your mother sent Scott here without his dad knowing, but he shouldn't be too upset. I mean, from what you've said, the boy was far better off here than in Kansas, right?"

"That's for sure."

"Hey!" said Scott sharply, clapping his hands three times. "You're doing it again; talking like I'm not here. But I agree. I am far better off here than in Kansas."

Tammie apologized, "Sorry, Scott. I didn't mean to do that." Turning to Todd, she asked, "Why are you worried? Am I missing something?"

"Remember, Charles and I haven't talked in a mighty long time," replied Todd, squirming uneasily.

"Yeah, I know, but don't you think it's about time? I mean, I don't know exactly what caused the problem between you two, but haven't you taken things to the extreme?"

"Charles was in love with a girl who was in love with me," Todd explained. "I didn't want to marry her. We had an argument and I left. Charles never forgave me."

Runt hopped up into the glider and laid his head on Todd's knee, whining; his large, mournful eyes pleading.

Scott prided himself on being able to figure out people by their expressions, regardless of what they said, and knew his uncle was hiding something.

Tammie wasn't fooled either. She stood, hands on hips, ogling at Todd as if he were a specimen in a laboratory test

146

tube. "I don't buy it. There's something else, something you're not saying."

"I don't know what you mean." Todd climbed out of the glider, rubbing his head. Crossing over to the doorway, he regarded the night sky. Getting Scott's attention, he said, "I need a crescent wrench. Would you find Jo-Go and borrow one for me?"

"Sure! A cres-cent wrench."

"You said it right. Jo-Go will know what you mean."

Scott signed 'okay.' He figured this was his uncle's way of getting him out of the picture, so they could talk about stuff they didn't want him to know.

What's Uncle Todd's secret? Maybe Tammie could be convinced to share it later.

Scott strolled to the ranch house and had just stepped on the porch when someone grabbed him from behind, picked him up, and set him back down on the ground. He turned to see Jo-Go grinning like the cookie monster that had just snatched something.

"You scared me!"

Jo-Go guffawed. "Sorry 'bout that."

"That's all right. Uncle Todd needs a cres-cent wrench."

"Well, you came to the right person." Jo-Go motioned for Scott to follow him out to the truck.

"My dad is coming."

Jo-Go stopped and faced him so he could see him answer.

"I know."

"Why are my uncle and dad not friends?"

"I never met your dad, but I understand he and your uncle had a big argument."

"I know." Scott hesitated a moment. There was a question he had to ask. He focused on Jo-Go. "Do you know why?"

"Aah…" Jo-Go just stared at him, apparently not knowing what to say.

"You do, don't you? Was it about my mother?"

Jo-Go reached behind the seat of the pickup, pulled out the wrench, and handed it to him. "For a guy who can't hear, you don't miss much, do you?"

Scott just lifted his shoulders and let them flop. That was all the answer he needed. *Still, that's not the whole story. There's more to it. There had to be. Why had that created such a wedge between them for so long?*

Scott thought about this as he returned to the hangar. Upon entering, he saw Tammie's lips say, "Sounds like you and your brother have some talking to do."

"Yeah," said Todd, "guess you're right."

Tammie rubbed his back. "Well, if you need a character reference or something, let me know."

"Thanks."

As Tammie left, she gave Scott a little hug. He felt her unconditional love clear to his bones as he handed his uncle the wrench.

"Thanks."

As Todd climbed back into the pilot's seat, Runt, who had been by the hangar door watching Scott, leaped back into the rear and reached over to console him with a lick on the ear.

Todd sat sideways in the seat and patted the dog on the head. Probably unaware that Scott could see him, he said, "'Fraid I'm going to need more than a character reference for this one, ol' buddy."

Runt cocked his head, tongue hanging out, then lifted his ears into an erect position as if he understood every word.

"What more do you need?" Scott asked curiously.

"Don't pay any attention to me." Todd laughed nervously. "I'm just babbling." He reached for his pills again. This time, he took one.

A Secret Revealed

Scott and his uncle sat nervously, side by side, waiting, in the living room of the ranch house. Runt was wedged between them, eyeing first one, then the other, as if puzzled by their behavior.

Suddenly, there was a knock at the front door. Runt's ears went up. He barked once and lunged, wagging his tail, as if waiting to greet an old friend.

With a pounding heart, Scott rushed over and flung the door open. "Dad!"

His dad gave him a big bear hug. Then signing and speaking, he said, "You look different. You have grown!"

"Dad, I have missed you!"

Charles Schroeder grabbed him by the shoulders and pushed him back at arm's length. "And I have missed you."

Jo-Go stepped in from the hallway and shook hands. "I'm Joseph Goens. Most folks just call me Jo-Go, and this is my wife, Tammie."

"Charles, welcome to our home," Tammie said, offering her hand.

"Yeah, you certainly are," Jo-Go agreed. "Make yourself at home. Scott will take care of you."

As Jo-Go and Tammie left, Scott grabbed his dad's arm. "Come." He tugged him into the living room.

Todd stood as they entered and greeted his brother with an outstretched hand.

"Why?" demanded Charles, ignoring the gesture. "Why did you let Mother send him here? Did you forget our agreement that you would stay out of our lives?"

Todd dropped his hand and snorted. "Your ultimatum, you mean. You never gave me a chance to agree."

"All right, so what did you do?" Charles' scowl deepened. "You waited until I was gone, then conspired to bring him here. For what purpose?"

"Conspired?!" Todd flushed. "You didn't appear too concerned. You went out of the country and abandoned him."

Scott's head shot back and forth between the two men. This was not what he wanted. They hated each other because of him.

He stomped his foot. With tears filling his eyes, he yelled and signed angrily, bringing the edge of his right hand into

the palm of his left. "Stop! Stop! Talk—not fight!"

Shocked into silence, the two men froze mid-thought.

"You are brothers," said Scott, signing and speaking at the same time. "Do not hate each other because of me." He strode to a window, crossing his arms in defiance.

In a moment, he felt a hand on his shoulder. Charles gently turned him about and raised his son's chin. "Scott, you are not the cause."

"But you argue about me." Tears ran down his cheeks in rivulets.

His dad looked at Todd. "I have to travel. It's what I do."

"Do you know why Mother called me?" Todd asked. "Scott and his friend almost caused a major fire."

"I know. Ralston told me." Just then, Charles noticed the dog for the first time.

Runt rose from his place next to Scott's feet and nuzzled Charles' hand.

"Runt had no one to care for him," said Scott.

"Besides," added Todd, "if he had been left in Kansas, you know what Mother would've done."

"I can't believe it." Charles scratched Runt behind the ears. "Ralston sent this dog all the way here. It's absurd."

"You weren't around, and the dog was," Todd said, looking pale, and sat back down on the couch.

Whining, Runt nervously moved to the other side of Scott and watched them intently.

Annoyed, Scott thought, *What was it about being deaf that made people, even relatives, treat you as if you weren't there?*

"Look, Charles," Todd said, "you can provide material things, but sometimes it takes more than that."

"I know." Charles's speech became slower as he took a seat in a chair facing his brother. "That's why we went to Kansas. I had hoped Mother would at least—I had not expected to be gone so long."

Fumbling into his jacket pocket, Todd pulled out a little bottle, shook out a pill, and popped it into his mouth.

"What're you taking?" Charles peered at him. "Are you all right?"

"Nitroglycerin."

"What! You mean you—"

"Yeah, I have a heart condition," Todd admitted.

"Why didn't you tell me?"

Scott stepped across the room to stand next to his uncle. "He didn't tell anybody until he had to."

"Why would I? So everyone could feel sorry for me? And remember, we haven't been talking much lately."

"Hey, little brother! Regardless, I have a right to know."

Scott sat on the arm of his uncle's chair. It wasn't hard to realize how his uncle felt. Most people are kind to folks with a handicap, but you could always see the pity in their eyes. He had experienced it too often.

Todd, who until that moment had not looked directly at

his brother, locked eyes with Charles. "There's something else I've wanted to say. About what happened… Well, I was unfair. And the funeral! I wasn't aware of it until—"

"I know, I know," Charles murmured. "I should have made a greater effort to find you."

Scott knew they were talking about his mom.

Charles hesitated for a few heartbeats, then tilted his head at Scott. "It would seem he inherited the best of everything in our family."

The brothers looked at each other and chuckled.

Scott looked from man to man before the truth hit him like a boulder. He gasped as if the wind had just been knocked out of him, then turned to stare out the window.

Finally, he knew their secret. With heart pounding, he felt the blood rushing to his head. In fact, the more he thought about it, the less of a secret it seemed. *Unbelievable. I had been lied to my entire life.*

He remembered how puzzling his grandmother's comment had been when they had first met; something about "the sins of the father were forgiven as seen in the son." Then there was the time he had looked through the window and saw his dad and grandmother argue about him seeing someone and he had thought, *Why?*

Why would an uncle I knew nothing about already have my picture and know all about me? Why would he take me in, look after me, and treat me like a son? Why had Dad been so angry with

Uncle Todd? There had been more to it than just a fight over Mom. The pieces all fit. The answer was obvious.

Soul searching amidst the blackness of the night. Something. Something, like an invisible phantom was twisting his stomach into knots. *I actually have* two *dads. Impossible.* He regarded first his dad, then Uncle Todd. *Mom must have loved them both. But does it really matter who my true dad is? Let the past be the past.*

He moved over to the man he had always known as his dad and shook his arm for attention. "There are things we must talk about."

Charles gently cuffed him on the ear. "We will. There is plenty of time."

Scott reluctantly agreed. He realized this was not the best time for a father/son talk. He signed 'okay,' then said, "Still, I want you to know I'm glad you're here."

His dad told him, "You know, your grandmother is not as clever as she thinks. When you weren't home after about the third time I called, things were beginning to smell fishy."

Scott cocked his head. "What do you mean?"

"Something was not right," said Charles, speaking slowly for Scott's benefit. "When Ralston told me what happened, he gave me Todd's address." He looked over at his brother. "You know, I think Mother planned this whole thing. She knew I would find out where Scott was. I think she wanted me to be forced into talking with you without involving her."

"That would be just like her," agreed Todd. "Well, it worked. Sometimes we don't give her enough credit when it comes to scheming in order to accomplish her intentions."

Charles said nothing for a moment, then motioned at Scott. "But she's never been good with kids."

"Yeah, I remember," said Todd, reminiscing.

All at once, Charles clapped a hand on Scott's shoulder. "Son, I've come to take you home."

"No, not yet!" Scott shook his head, pleading, "Uncle Todd?! The gymnastics competition!"

Signaling him to stop, Charles said, "Let me finish! We'll stay for a while, okay?"

"At least two weeks," insisted Scott.

"Why?"

"I compete in gymnastics this weekend. Uncle Todd races his glider next weekend."

Todd was amused with his brother's perplexed expression. "We've been kind of busy."

"Apparently." Charles put his arm around Scott. "He wrote that he was taking gymnastics again. I might be able to arrange to stay; that is if your friends can put up with me that long." He looked up as Tammie and Jo-Go breached the doorway.

"You're more than welcome."

"Thanks," said Charles, bowing his head slightly in appreciation. Addressing Scott, he tried to explain, "To finish what I was about to say, when I talk about home, I don't mean Kansas."

With that, he had everyone's attention

"That's my surprise." Charles clapped his hands. "There was an opening for a co-ordinator. I applied for it and got it."

"You, a co-or-di-na-tor?" said Scott, stumbling over the word.

"Afraid so. This means you'll have to put up with me being around a lot."

"Yes!" Scott squealed, jumping up and down. Abruptly, he stopped, stock-still. There was too much happening all at once. "Where is home?"

"First, you must understand. This means you're *not* going to hop on a borrowed bike and chase a truck down a freeway."

Scott touched the side of his face with the tips of his fingers. "I know."

"And you're *not* going to fire off a rocket in the middle of a city park."

Scott grimaced, impatiently. "Dad! I understand! Tell me! Where is home?"

"You've met the man I'm going to replace. In fact, you've been in his office; the office that will now be mine."

Scott rattled his brain. Then, like a distant glow in the dark of night, he began to understand.

"Home!" he exclaimed. "We're going home!"

"Exactly."

"Hold on!" shouted Todd. "You've lost me. What are you talking about?"

"We're going back to Texas," said Charles.

Scott tackled his dad in a hug. *I can work out with my friends on the gymnastics team again! And tell them about my summer experiences! We're actually going home!* But then another thought crossed his mind. He looked from Todd to Tammie to Jo-Go and felt a strange uneasiness. *Perhaps, my new home should be here, in California.*

He stepped back and studied the two men, watching for unspoken communication between them. Maybe they could work something out like split families do. Maybe he could spend summers in California and go to school in Texas.

Tammie started out the door. "Hey, if you guys plan to stay up all night, I'll leave the teapot on."

"I think we can call it quits till morning," suggested Todd.

"Then, if you'll come with me," said Tammie to Charles, "I'll show you where the guest room is."

"Charles." Todd shook hands with his brother. "Tomorrow, I want to show you the fastest glider in the country."

"Sure thing."

Scott tugged on his dad's sleeve. "There is much to talk about."

"I know, son. We will tomorrow. I'm not going anywhere." Charles smiled at his hosts. "Tammie, thanks for your hospitality." Happily ruffling Scott's hair, he added, "Till morning."

Scott was elated to have him back. "Good night, Dad."

As Scott and Todd walked out on the porch, his uncle tapped him on the shoulder. "You go on to bed. I'll be along in a few minutes. I'm just going to stop by the hangar."

Scott was tired. He wanted to talk with his uncle as well, but not then. He signed 'good night' and made his way through the dark to the trailer.

Journey's End

Scott sat up with a start. Runt was tugging at his covers and had partly pulled them to the floor. Rubbing his eyes, he squinted in the darkness of the trailer. In the dim glow of the night-light, everything appeared quite normal. *What has gotten Runt so riled??*

Scott noticed his uncle stirring in his bed on the other side of the room. The dog must have been barking as well.

Runt raced to the door and scratched on the paneling.

Scott threw his covers to the side. His uncle appeared to be muttering to himself as he dropped his feet to the floor. Hopping out of bed, Scott stumbled toward the door, opened it, and flipped on the outside light.

Runt bounded out into the night. Faintly wagging his tail, he barked at the hangar, then glanced back at Scott.

Todd ambled up from behind, scratching his head, mumbling something about, "That crazy dog."

A light flickered in the hangar's window. It did not register in Scott's brain for a full two seconds.

"Fire!" Grabbing his uncle's arm, he pointed at the hangar. "Fire!"

They raced back into the trailer. Scott struggled into his trousers and slipped on his shoes, while Todd put on his boots and snatched his shirt.

Together, they dashed back out of the trailer. Todd grabbed Scott's arm and motioned toward the ranch house as he ran into the office.

Though Scott didn't see what his uncle said, he knew what was wanted. He ran up the steps to the front door of the ranch house and pounded on the door. "Fire!" He pounded on the door again and repeated, "Fire!"

Lights went on, but Scott didn't wait. He grabbed a garden hose as Charles and Jo-Go raced out the front door.

Quickly, Scott connected the hose to an outside spigot, turned on the water, and raced to the front of the hangar, tugging the end of the garden hose behind him.

Todd was fumbling with the keys. He unlocked the door and rolled it open, then reached for the fire extinguisher.

A cloud of smoke sent both reeling.

Todd charged forward with the fire extinguisher.

Scott crouched low, tugging on the hose and spraying.

Runt barked excitedly, darting back and forth, from one area to another.

Hungry flames crept along the inside walls. They had already engulfed one wall and were licking at the tail of a sailplane.

While Todd attacked the flames with the extinguisher, Scott crouched low to avoid the smoke. He jerked the garden hose in until it would let him go no further. Twisting the nozzle, he made the water spray as far as possible.

Nevertheless, the flames increased and spread toward the storage closet.

Todd worked the extinguisher until it ran out of chemicals, then flung it to the side and began fumbling with the guide lines that held the Adventurer.

Scott could see what his uncle was doing and knew it was the only way to save the glider.

Throwing down the hose, Scott scrambled for the lines on the opposite side of the aircraft. He ignored his uncle who was frantically motioning at him to move away.

Todd yanked one line loose and started toward another. He dropped to the floor to avoid the smoke and crawled to a tie, struggling to undo it.

Scott crawled to the last tie on the opposite side. Though his eyes were stinging from the smoke, he rose halfway to his feet, staggered to the back of one wing, and pushed. His uncle moved to the other wing and did the same.

As the glider rolled forward, his uncle's side stopped moving.

Scott dropped to the floor, rubbing his eyes to clear some of the stinging smoke from them, and glanced over to see what was happening.

Todd had tripped over a mooring and fell. He was struggling to pull himself up. But before he could get to his feet, he grabbed his chest and dropped back to the floor.

Scott screamed, "No!" Half-blinded by the smoke, he scrambled to his uncle's side and grabbed Todd's arm, jerking on it with all his strength.

"Come on!" he shouted. "Come on!"

With Scott's help, Todd crawled a little way before collapsing completely.

Runt grabbed a sleeve of Todd's robe between his teeth and tugged viciously. Yet, despite all efforts, Todd wasn't moving. The dog dropped the sleeve and licked his face. Todd grasped his chest; his breath escaping in short quick gasps.

Scott grabbed Todd's arm and pulled with every ounce of strength he had.

Todd blurted out, "My pills! The trailer!"

"Got to get you out, first," yelled Scott.

Coughing from the smoke, Scott dropped Todd's arm and grabbed the back of his shirt, leaned backwards with all his might and pulled his uncle to the tarmac. Frantically trying to wipe the smoke out of his eyes, he screamed, "Help!

Somebody help!"

There was no one. The others were struggling with a hose at the rear of the hangar where the flames were shooting through the roof.

The strobing lights of a fire tanker assailed him. The firemen had connected a hose and were yanking it toward the hangar's entrance.

Scott yelled and pointed, "My uncle! He needs help!"

He raced ahead of the firemen, back to the hangar's entrance where Todd lay unmoving and not breathing.

The flames had engulfed another wall and were spreading among the overhead beams. One trainer was smothered in flames, and the fire was eating its way along the tail of another glider.

A pair of arms jerked him out of the way as the firemen rushed past him.

He struggled, screaming, "Let go!"

An explosion ripped through one corner of the structure where fuel for the Piper Cub was kept. The firemen backed out the door as a tremendous flash of fire and smoke engulfed the entire hangar.

Scott screamed and shook all over, "No!" He abruptly tore loose from the fireman's grasp and ran from the death and destruction. He had no idea where, he just had to go somewhere, anywhere.

Stumbling through the woods, he fell, got up, and ran

again. Struggling through some brush, he stepped in a hole and tripped over a stump, landing against the trunk of a tree.

Covering his eyes, he sobbed.

Years before, there had been another explosion. He had been thrown from a car as it tumbled down the side of a mountain. There had been the smell of smoke, the flames, the loneliness. That was followed by voiceless faces, pitying stares, and the hospital smell of medicines and antiseptics. He had learned then what it was like to feel alone among strangers.

He was alone now.

He cried out, "Dad! Dad! Where are you?"

"I'm here, son. I'm here," replied a breathless voice.

"Dad!"

"You all right?"

"Uncle Todd... Runt... they..."

Charles grabbed Scott by the shoulders and pulled him into a position facing him. In the light of the hangar's ascending flames, he cupped Scott's tear-streaked face. "Scott! Scott! You weren't looking at me and *heard* what I said!"

Scott looked at his dad in amazement. "I-I did!" *The doctors' prediction had finally come true!* His head snapped in the direction of the fiery hangar. "The flames! I hear them! Dad! The hangar!"

His dad's face was streaked with grime. In a choking voice, he whispered, "I know, son. It's too late."

Scott buried his face in his dad's shirt.

Another fire tanker arrived on the scene, as well as the Rescue Squad. Firemen scrambled to unload the equipment. Diligently, with arms wrapped around another fire hose, they doused the structure. EMTs surrounded Todd, pounding his chest, giving him oxygen. Scott knew his uncle was gone. *But where is Runt?*

Charles choked out a sob; tears flowed streaking his face. Together, they sat on the forest floor, arm in arm, observing the chaos as the flaming structure fell into a glowing heap of rubble.

★ ★ ★

As dawn arrived, Todd had been taken away and the hangar was a smoldering mess. The fire engines, the police, the onlookers, all had left. Jo-Go and Tammie had long ago dragged themselves back into the ranch house while Scott and his dad continued to sit near the edge of the runway.

Scott stared at the blackened ruins. *Where's Runt? Could he have escaped the fire? If so, he might be hiding in the woods.* Pulling the whistle out from beneath his shirt, Scott got to his feet and blew on it as long and as hard as he could.

No response.

Contemplating what was left of the hangar, whiffs of smoke ascended into the sky. *Runt would not have left Todd's side.* Deflated, he sat back down next to his dad.

The Fire Marshall had already been there and stated that a short in an electric heater had caused the fire. In the cooler evenings, air flowed down from the mountains. Scott remembered how his uncle would flip on the heater to ward off the chill. He must have been really tired when he left the hangar to have forgotten about it.

Standing on the edge of the disaster, searching the place where he had last seen Todd and Runt, with a muffled sob, he dropped his head into his hands. There had been no time to say goodbye. He never had the chance to tell Todd that he knew his secret.

Scott felt his dad's arm on his shoulder and looked up.

Charles had been his dad for thirteen years. It was a little late to start thinking of him as an uncle. He wanted to tell him he knew their secret, to just blurt out that it didn't matter, but he didn't know how to begin.

A sparrow chirped from the branch of a scraggly pine. Scott listened to its clear, precise sounds. He looked in its direction. "That's a bird!"

Charles, staring at the devastation, absently said, "There's a world of sound around that you haven't heard in a long time." He spun about and faced Scott. "Son, there are things I need to tell you. They concern your uncle and—"

"No, Dad." Scott took in his dad's tired eyes and worried face.

Finally, the truth.

"Don't! I already figured it out, and it doesn't make any difference."

"What?!"

Scott gripped his dad's hands. "Uncle Todd was much more than just my uncle, wasn't he?"

"But how—"

"Dad, when you live in a world of silence, you learn to watch and think, maybe more clearly than you would otherwise."

Scott squeezed harder to get his attention. "Hey, look. It doesn't matter."

His dad clasped his hand in return, then put his arm around Scott's shoulder and choked a little as he added, "To me, you have always been my son and always will be."

Scott hugged him fiercely. "And you've always been my dad. I don't think I could ever call you 'Uncle.'"

Together, they walked along the runway.

Neither looking at one another, his dad said, "Tonight you've changed. You're not just a kid anymore."

"I don't feel changed."

"But you have. Don't worry. It's a good change." He haltingly looked back at what was left of the burned structure and added, "It's time to go."

"First, there's something I need to do." Scott wiped a sleeve across his face. With a slight limp, he walked toward the smoldering debris. The ankle bothered him, but there

was one last debt he owed his friend. Rambling through the roofless structure of the hangar, he knocked pieces of charred material out of his way.

"Be careful!" cautioned his dad. "Some of it's still hot."

Out of habit, Scott gestured an okay.

Near the remains of the Adventurer, he found what he was looking for and dropped to his knees. Gently, he picked up the singed body of the small German shepherd. With tears rolling down his face, he carried it out of the rubble.

There was a hill near a far corner of the airfield. From it could be seen the freeway with the trucks and rigs passing by—a good place for Runt's final resting place.

Scott's dad went to the ranch house and returned with a shovel. They took turns digging a small grave. After laying Runt's body in it, the two of them created a mound of dirt and covered it with stones. Then, they made a small wooden cross.

"Dad," said Scott, "I want to stay a minute."

Charles nodded. "Meet you back down on the road."

Scott stood quietly a moment, looking down at the stones.

"Don't know exactly what to say," he began. "I'm going to miss you. Guess the most I can say is thanks. Thanks for being my friend."

He wiped his face with the sleeve of his shirt. "If you come across my uncle—rather—my dad, take care of him. I know the two of you would be happy together." He turned and, with one last glance over his shoulder, limped down the hill.

The man Scott had always known as his dad waited at the bottom.

"You all right?" he asked.

"Think so," replied Scott.

They strolled slowly back toward the house. At the steps leading to the front porch, Scott stopped and glanced up at a movement in the sky.

He grabbed his father's arm.

"Look!"

The sun reflected from a bright, red glider that circled above. It had found a thermo and rode the warm air currents. Higher and higher it climbed until it disappeared over the crest of a mountain.

Scott smiled slightly as he thought of his two guardian angels, 'Uncle' Todd and Runt. "Everything's going to be all right, Dad. I know it will."

Arm in arm, they climbed the stairs together.

The End

A SOLDIER'S EMBRACE

Stories by

NADINE GORDIMER

The Viking Press   New York

First published in 1980 by The Viking Press
625 Madison Avenue, New York, N.Y. 10022
Published simultaneously in Canada by
Penguin Books Canada Limited

LIBRARY OF CONGRESS CATALOGING IN PUBLICATION DATA
Gordimer, Nadine.
A soldier's embrace.
I. Title.
PZ4.G66Sp   [PR9369.3.G6]   823   79-56266
ISBN 0-670-65638-0

Printed in the United States of America
Set in Plantin

"A Soldier's Embrace" and "A Lion on the Freeway" appeared originally in *Harper's;* "Oral History"
in *Playboy;* "Town and Country Lovers" in *The
New Yorker* under the title "City Lovers."

CONTENTS

For Paule Taramasco

A SOLDIER'S EMBRACE

The day the cease-fire was signed she was caught in a crowd. Peasant boys from Europe who had made up the colonial army and freedom fighters whose column had marched into town were staggering about together outside the barracks, not three blocks from her house in whose rooms, for ten years, she had heard the blurred parade-ground bellow of colonial troops being trained to kill and be killed.

The men weren't drunk. They linked and swayed across the street; because all that had come to a stop, everything *had* to come to a stop: they surrounded cars, bicycles, vans, nannies with children, women with loaves of bread or basins of mangoes on their heads, a road gang with picks and shovels, a Coca-Cola truck, an old man with a barrow who bought bottles and bones. They were grinning and laughing amazement. That it could be: there they were, bumping into each other's bodies in joy, looking into each other's rough faces, all eyes crescent-shaped, brimming greeting. The words were in languages not mutually comprehensible, but the cries were new, a whooping and crowing all understood. She was bumped and jostled and she let go, stopped trying to move in any self-determined direction. There were two soldiers in front of her, blocking her off by their clumsy embrace (how do you do it, how do you do what you've never done before) and the embrace opened like a door and took her in—a pink hand with bitten nails grasping her right arm, a black hand with a big-dialled watch and thong bracelet pulling at her left elbow. Their three heads collided gaily, musk of sweat and tang of strong sweet soap clapped a mask to her nose and mouth. They all gasped with delicious shock. They were saying things to each other. She put up an arm round each neck, the rough pile of an army haircut on one side, the soft negro hair on the other, and kissed them both on the cheek. The embrace broke. The crowd wove her away behind backs, arms, jogging heads; she was returned to and took up the will of her direction again—she was walking home from

8

the post office, where she had just sent a telegram to relatives abroad: ALL CALM DON'T WORRY.

The lawyer came back early from his offices because the courts were not sitting although the official celebration holiday was not until next day. He described to his wife the rally before the Town Hall, which he had watched from the office-building balcony. One of the guerilla leaders (not the most important; he on whose head the biggest price had been laid would not venture so soon and deep into the territory so newly won) had spoken for two hours from the balcony of the Town Hall. 'Brilliant. Their jaws dropped. Brilliant. They've never heard anything on that level: precise, reasoned—none of them would ever have believed it possible, out of the bush. You should have seen de Poorteer's face. He'd like to be able to get up and open his mouth like that. And be listened to like that...' The Governor's handicap did not even bring the sympathy accorded to a stammer; he paused and gulped between words. The blacks had always used a portmanteau name for him that meant the-crane-who-is-trying-to-swallow-the-bullfrog.

One of the members of the black underground organization that could now come out in brass-band support of the freedom fighters had recognized the lawyer across from the official balcony and given him the freedom fighters' salute. The lawyer joked about it, miming, full of pride. 'You should have been there— should have seen him, up there in the official party. I told you— really—you ought to have come to town with me this morning.'

'And what did you do?' She wanted to assemble all details.

'Oh I gave the salute in return, chaps in the street saluted me... everybody was doing it. It was marvellous. And the police standing by; just to think, last month—only last week—you'd have been arrested.'

'Like thumbing your nose at them,' she said, smiling.

'Did anything go on around here?'

'Muchanga was afraid to go out all day. He wouldn't even run up to the post office for me!' Their servant had come to them

9

many years ago, from service in the house of her father, a colonial official in the Treasury.

'But there was no excitement?'

She told him: 'The soldiers and some freedom fighters mingled outside the barracks. I got caught for a minute or two. They were dancing about; you couldn't get through. All very good-natured. —Oh, I sent the cable.'

An accolade, one side a white cheek, the other a black. The white one she kissed on the left cheek, the black one on the right cheek, as if these were two sides of one face.

That vision, version, was like a poster; the sort of thing that was soon peeling off dirty shopfronts and bus shelters while the months of wrangling talks preliminary to the take-over by the black government went by.

To begin with, the cheek was not white but pale or rather sallow, the poor boy's pallor of winter in Europe (that draft must have only just arrived and not yet seen service) with homesick pimples sliced off by the discipline of an army razor. And the cheek was not black but opaque peat-dark, waxed with sweat round the plump contours of the nostril. As if she could return to the moment again, she saw what she had not consciously noted: there had been a narrow pink strip in the darkness near the ear, the sort of tender stripe of healed flesh revealed when a scab is nicked off a little before it is ripe. The scab must have come away that morning: the young man picked at it in the troop carrier or truck (whatever it was the freedom fighters had; the colony had been told for years that they were supplied by the Chinese and Russians indiscriminately) on the way to enter the capital in triumph.

According to newspaper reports, the day would have ended for the two young soldiers in drunkenness and whoring. She was, apparently, not yet too old to belong to the soldier's embrace of all that a land-mine in the bush might have exploded for ever. That was one version of the incident. Another: the opportunity taken by a woman not young enough to be clasped in the arms of the one who (same newspaper, while the war was on, expressing the fears of the colonists for their women) would be expected to rape her.

She considered this version.

She had not kissed on the mouth, she had not sought anonymous lips and tongues in the licence of festival. Yet she had kissed. Watching herself again, she knew that. She had—god knows why —kissed them on either cheek, his left, his right. It was deliberate, if a swift impulse: she had distinctly made the move.

She did not tell what happened not because her husband would suspect licence in her, but because he would see her—born and brought up in the country as the daughter of an enlightened white colonial official, married to a white liberal lawyer well known for his defence of blacks in political trials—as giving free expression to liberal principles.

She had not told, she did not know what had happened.

She thought of a time long ago when a school camp had gone to the sea and immediately on arrival everyone had run down to the beach from the train, tripping and tearing over sand dunes of wild fig, aghast with ecstatic shock at the meeting with the water.

De Poorteer was recalled and the lawyer remarked to one of their black friends, 'The crane has choked on the bullfrog. I hear that's what they're saying in the Quarter.'

The priest who came from the black slum that had always been known simply by that anonymous term did not respond with any sort of glee. His reserve implied it was easy to celebrate; there were people who 'shouted freedom too loud all of a sudden'.

The lawyer and his wife understood: Father Mulumbua was one who had shouted freedom when it was dangerous to do so, and gone to prison several times for it, while certain people, now on the Interim Council set up to run the country until the new government took over, had kept silent. He named a few, but reluctantly. Enough to confirm their own suspicions—men who perhaps had made some deal with the colonial power to place its interests first, no matter what sort of government might emerge from the new constitution? Yet when the couple plunged into discussion their friend left them talking to each other while he drank his beer and gazed, frowning as if at a headache or because the sunset light hurt his eyes behind his spectacles, round her huge-leaved tropical plants that bowered the terrace in cool humidity.

They had always been rather proud of their friendship with him, this man in a cassock who wore a clenched fist carved of local ebony as well as a silver cross round his neck. His black face was habitually stern—a high seriousness balanced by sudden splurting laughter when they used to tease him over the fist—but never inattentively ill-at-ease.

'What was the matter?' She answered herself; 'I had the feeling he didn't want to come here.' She was using a paper handkerchief dipped in gin to wipe greenfly off the back of a pale new leaf that had shaken itself from its folds like a cut-out paper lantern.

'Good lord, he's been here hundreds of times.'

'—Before, yes.'

What things were they saying?

With the shouting in the street and the swaying of the crowd, the sweet powerful presence that confused the senses so that sound, sight, stink (sweat, cheap soap) ran into one tremendous sensation, she could not make out words that came so easily.

Not even what she herself must have said.

A few wealthy white men who had been boastful in their support of the colonial war and knew they would be marked down by the blacks as arch exploiters, left at once. Good riddance, as the lawyer and his wife remarked. Many ordinary white people who had lived contentedly, without questioning its actions, under the colonial government, now expressed an enthusiastic intention to help build a nation, as the newspapers put it. The lawyer's wife's neighbourhood butcher was one. 'I don't mind blacks.' He was expansive with her, in his shop that he had occupied for twelve years on a licence available only to white people. 'Makes no difference to me who you are so long as you're honest.' Next to a chart showing a beast mapped according to the cuts of meat it provided, he had hung a picture of the most important leader of the freedom fighters, expected to be first President. People like the butcher turned out with their babies clutching pennants when the leader drove through the town from the airport.

There were incidents (newspaper euphemism again) in the Quarter. It was to be expected. Political factions, tribally based, who had not fought the war, wanted to share power with the freedom fighters' Party. Muchanga no longer went down to the Quarter on his day off. His friends came to see him and sat privately on their hunkers near the garden compost heap. The ugly mansions of the rich who had fled stood empty on the bluff above the sea, but it was said they would make money out of them yet —they would be bought as ambassadorial residences when independence came, and with it many black and yellow diplomats. Zealots who claimed they belonged to the Party burned shops and houses of the poorer whites who lived, as the lawyer said, 'in the inevitable echelon of colonial society', closest to the Quarter. A house in the lawyer's street was noticed by his wife to be accommodating what was certainly one of those families, in the outhouses; green nylon curtains had appeared at the garage window, she reported. The suburb was pleasantly overgrown and well-to-do; no one rich, just white professional people and professors from the university. The barracks was empty now, except for an old man with a stump and a police uniform stripped of insignia, a friend of Muchanga, it turned out, who sat on a beer-crate at the gates. He had lost his job as night-watchman when one of the rich people went away, and was glad to have work.

The street had been perfectly quiet; except for that first day.

The fingernails she sometimes still saw clearly were bitten down until embedded in a thin line of dirt all round, in the pink blunt fingers. The thumb and thick fingertips were turned back coarsely even while grasping her. Such hands had never been allowed to take possession. They were permanently raw, so young, from unloading coal, digging potatoes from the frozen Northern Hemisphere, washing hotel dishes. He had not been killed, and now that day of the cease-fire was over he would be delivered back across the sea to the docks, the stony farm, the scullery of the grand hotel. He would have to do anything he could get. There was unemployment in Europe where he had returned, the army didn't need all the young men any more.

A great friend of the lawyer and his wife, Chipande, was coming home from exile. They heard over the radio he was expected, accompanying the future President as confidential secretary, and they waited to hear from him.

The lawyer put up his feet on the empty chair where the priest had sat, shifting it to a comfortable position by hooking his toes, free in sandals, through the slats. 'Imagine, Chipande!' Chipande had been almost a protégé—but they didn't like the term, it smacked of patronage. Tall, cocky, casual Chipande, a boy from the slummiest part of the Quarter, was recommended by the White Fathers' Mission (was it by Father Mulumbua himself?— the lawyer thought so, his wife was not sure they remembered correctly) as a bright kid who wanted to be articled to a lawyer. That was asking a lot, in those days—nine years ago. He never finished his apprenticeship because while he and his employer were soon close friends, and the kid picked up political theories from the books in the house he made free of, he became so involved in politics that he had to skip the country one jump ahead of a detention order signed by the crane-who-was-trying-to-swallow-the-bullfrog.

After two weeks, the lawyer phoned the offices the guerilla-movement-become-Party had set up openly in the town but apparently Chipande had an office in the former colonial secretariat. There he had a secretary of his own; he wasn't easy to reach. The lawyer left a message. The lawyer and his wife saw from the newspaper pictures he hadn't changed much: he had a beard and had adopted the Muslim cap favoured by political circles in exile on the East Coast.